RESCUING
THE ROYAL
RUNAWAY BRIDE

RESCUING THE ROYAL RUNAWAY BRIDE

ALLY BLAKE

MILLS & BOON

First published in Great Britain 2018
by Mills & Boon, an imprint of HarperCollins*Publishers*
1 London Bridge Street, London, SE1 9GF

Large Print edition 2018

ISBN: 978-0-263-07415-4

For my husband, Mark,
who loves nothing more than
looking to the stars.

CHAPTER ONE

THE DAY COULD not be more perfect for a royal wedding, thought Will as his open-topped hire car chewed up miles of undulating Vallemontian roads.

The sky was a cerulean-blue dome. Clusters of puffy white cumuli hovered over snow-dusted mountains and dotted shadows over rolling green hills filling the valley that gave the small European principality its name.

By Will's calculations, snow should fall on the valley any day. Instead, the delicate bite of a warm sun cut through the washed-clean feeling that came after lashings of rain. It was as if the influential Vallemontian royal family had wished for it to be so, and so it was.

But Will Darcy did not believe in wishes. He believed in the human eye's ability to find millions of colours in a drop of light; the resultant heat of distantly burning stars; that weather forecasting was an inexact science.

This coming from an astronomer; his field truly a game of extrapolation, using ancient evidence to build current theory, relying on calculations that pushed against the edges of the range of known values. One had to be part cowboy, part explorer, part decoder, idealist and seer to do well in the field—something he'd addressed as the keynote speaker at the Space and Time Forum in London the night before.

It had been a late night too. Hence the fact he'd flown into Vallemont only that morning, and would arrive at the palace just as the ceremony was about to start.

The delayed flight had also given him plenty of opportunity to back out if need be. There was the lecture on worm holes he was due to give at the University of Amsterdam a few days from now, after all. The podcast with newyorker.com. The notes from his editor on the second edition of his graduate-level astronomy textbook due any day. And then there was the virtual-reality game set in the Orion Nebula for which he was both investor and technical advisor.

Reasons enough to forgo the trip.

But only one reason to get on that plane.

To see his old friend tie the knot.

A day for knots, Will thought, choosing to ignore the one that had formed overnight in his belly at the thought of what this day might bring.

He pressed down on the accelerator on the neat little convertible his assistant had hired for him in the hope he might "realise how damn lucky he was and take a moment to enjoy himself". The chill wind ruffled his hair as he zoomed through the bucolic countryside until the road narrowed, heralding yet another idyllic Arcadian village.

Around a tight bend and he was in the thick of it—tightly winding cobblestone streets dotted with gaslight-style street lamps, stone houses with thatched roofs tucked tightly together and wedged into the side of a steep hill, their windowsills abundant with brightly coloured flowers; history in crumbling stone walls, mossy pavements and the occasional brass sign telling of times past.

The engine on the low-slung sports model growled as Will changed down a gear. The suspension knocked his teeth together as it struggled against the ancient stone beneath, but it was all he could do to avoid the crowd spilling from the thin footpaths onto the road.

Festive they were. All smiles as they headed

to pubs and parks and lounge rooms all over the country to watch the wedding on television. Pink and gold ribbons had been strung across the road. Handmade banners flapped from weathervanes. Pink flower petals covered the footpaths and floated in tiny puddles.

All because Will's oldest friend, Hugo, was getting married to some woman named Mercedes Gray Leonine, no less. Though those who had strung the ribbons and scattered the petals knew the guy as Prince Alessandro Hugo Giordano.

Then the roadway cleared and Will aimed for a stone bridge crossing the rocky river that trapped the village against the hillside and hit open space again.

It was all so very green, rain having brought a lush overabundance, shine and glisten as far as the eye could see.

And on he drove. Until he reached a tunnel of trees running parallel to the river.

Glimpses of fields pushing into the distance sneaked through the dark foliage. The ever-present mountains cast cool shadows through the sunshine. And, if his GPS wasn't glitching, any moment to the east…

There. Sunlight bounced off arched windows

and turned pale sandstone turrets into rose-gold. Pink and gold banners flapped high in the breeze while the Palace of Vallemont sat high and grand on its pretty bluff, like something out of a fairy tale.

And the knot in Will's stomach grew so that it pressed hard against his lungs.

The first time he'd been invited to the palace had been well over a decade before. Circumstances—by way of a skiing accident—had seen to it that he'd been forced to stay at his grandparents' mausoleum of a townhouse in London that summer, leaving his sister, Clair, to visit the royal family as Hugo's special guest on her own.

Only a few weeks later, Will's life had been irrevocably, tragically altered. The boy who'd already lost so much became a young man who'd lost everything. And Vallemont, this postcard-pretty part of the world, had been a throbbing bruise on his subconscious ever since.

Memories lifted and flurried. He'd handled things less than admirably at the time. This was his chance to put things right. He held the steering wheel tighter and kept moving forward.

The thicket filled out, the view narrowing to the curving tunnel of green and rutting muddy road that hadn't had the benefit of recent sunshine. A herd of sheep suddenly tripped and tumbled their way across the road.

Will slowed again, this time to a stop. He rested his elbow on the windowsill, his chin in his hand, his finger tapping against his bottom lip. If life wasn't so cruel, random and insensate, he might one day have attended a very different wedding in this storybook place. Not as a ghost from the groom's past, but as best man and brother, all in one.

He shook his head.

What ifs were not relevant. The world simply kept on turning. Day would dissolve into night. And tomorrow it would start all over again.

The last of the sheep skittered past, followed by a wizened old man in overalls holding a crook. He tipped his hat. Will returned with a salute. And then he and the knot in his belly were off again.

He kept his speed down as rain had dug deep grooves into the ancient mud and stone. The trees hung dangerously low over the road, dappling sunlight over the windscreen, shadow and light dancing across his hands, hindering his vision for a second, then—

Will slammed on the brakes. He gripped the wheel as the car fishtailed, mud spattering every which way, the engine squalling, the small tyres struggling to find purchase.

Then the car skidded to a jarring halt, momentum throwing him forward hard against the seatbelt, knocking his breath from his lungs. At which point the engine sputtered and died.

His chest burned from the impact of the belt. His fingers stung on the wheel. Blood rushed like an ocean behind his ears. Adrenaline poured hotly through his veins. And beneath it all his heart clanged in terror.

He'd heard a noise. He was sure of it. The growl and splutter had been punctuated with a thud.

Expecting carnage, axle damage from a fallen log, or, worse, a lone sheep thrown clear by the impact, Will opened his eyes.

Sunlight streaked through the thicket. Steam rose from the road. Wet leaves fell like confetti from a tree above. But there was no sheep in sight.

Instead, dead centre of his windscreen, stood a woman.

He blinked to make sure he wasn't imagining

her. So pale, sylph-like in the shadows of the dark, dank vegetation, she practically glowed.

As if in slow motion, a leaf fluttered from above to snag in a dark auburn curl dangling over her face. Another landed on a fair bare shoulder. Yet another snagged on the wide skirt of a voluminous pink dress three times bigger than she was.

Those were details that stampeded through Will's mind during the half-second it took him to leap from the car. The mud sluicing over the tops of his dress shoes and seeping into his socks mattered only so far as the fact it slowed him down.

"Where are you hurt?" he barked, running his hands through his hair to dampen the urge to run them over her.

Not that she seemed to notice. Her eyes remained closed, mouth downturned, black-streaked tears ran unstopped down her cheeks. And she trembled as if a strong gust of wind might whip her away.

Best case scenario was shock. Worst case... The thud still echoed against the back of his skull.

"Ma'am, I need you to look at me," he said, his voice louder now. It was the kind of voice that could silence a room full of jaded policy-makers. "Right now."

The woman flinched, her throat working. And then she opened her eyes.

They were enormous. Far too big for her face. Blue. Maybe green. Not easy to tell considering they were rimmed red and swollen with dark tears.

And every part of her vibrated a little more, from her clumpy eyelashes to the skirt of her elaborate dress. Standing there in the loaded silence, the hiss and tic of his cooling engine the only sound, he knew he'd never felt such energy pouring off a single person before. Like the sun's corona, it extended well beyond her physical body, impinging on anyone in its path.

He took what felt like a necessary step back as he said, "I cannot help you until you tell me whether you are hurt."

She let out one last head-to-toe quiver, then dragged in a breath. It seemed to do the trick as she blinked. Looked at his car. Lifted her hands into the air as if to balance. Pink diamonds dangling from her ears glinted softly as she shook her head. *No.*

Will breathed out, the sound not altogether together. Then, as relief broke the tension, anger tumbled through the rare breach in his faculties.

"Then what the holy hell were you doing jumping out in front of my car?"

The woman blinked at his outburst, her eyes becoming bigger still. Then her chin lifted, she seemed to grow an inch in height, and finally she found her voice. "I beg your pardon, but I did *not* jump out in front of your car."

Will baulked. The lilting, sing-song quality of the Vallemontian accent that he had not heard in person in years was resonant in every syllable. It took him back in time, making the ground beneath his feet unsteady.

He refocused. "Jump. Leap. Swan dive. It's all the same. You had to have heard me coming. My car engine isn't exactly subtle."

That earned him a surprisingly unladylike snort. "Subtle? It's a mid-life crisis incarnate. *You* should have been driving your overcompensation more slowly! Especially with the roads being as they are after the rain we've had."

"It's a rental," he shot back, then gave himself a swift mental kick for having risen to the bait. "Speed was not the issue here. The pertinent fact is that you chose to cross at a bend in the road shaded by thick foliage. You could have been killed. Or was that your intention? If so it was an obtuse plan. Nearly every person in the country is already at the palace or sitting by a TV to watch the royal wedding."

At that she winced, her pale face turning so much paler he could practically see the veins working beneath her skin. Then she broke eye contact, her chin dipping as she muttered, "My being right here, right now, was never part of any plan, I can assure you of that."

Okay. All right. Things had gone astray. Time to bring everything back to fundamentals. "So, just to be clear, I did not hit you."

She shook her head, dark red curls wobbling. "No, you did not."

"I could have sworn I heard a thud."

Her mouth twisted. Then she looked up at him from beneath long, clumping eyelashes. "When I saw you coming I did the only thing I could think to do. I threw a shoe at you."

"A shoe?"

"I'd have thrown both if I'd thought it would help. But alas, the other one is stuck."

"Stuck?" Will was aware he was beginning to sound like a parrot, but the late night, early morning, the knotty reality of being in Vallemont after all these years were beginning to take their toll.

He watched in mute interest as the woman gathered her dress and lifted it to show off skinny legs covered in pale pink stockings. One foot was bare. The other foot was nowhere to be seen—or, more precisely, was ankle-deep in mud.

Will glanced back at his car. Then up along the road ahead.

Time was ticking. Hugo's wedding was looming. Will wasn't sure of the protocol but he doubted a soon-to-be princess bride would be fashionably late.

The woman in pink was calmer now, the static having dulled to a mild buzz. Best of all she was unhurt, meaning she was not his problem.

Will did not do "people problems". His assistant, Natalie—a jolly, hardworking woman who performed miracles from a desk at home somewhere in the Midwest of the United States—was the only person in the world to whom he felt beholden and only because she told him every time they spoke that he should. Even then her efforts on his behalf were well-compensated.

He preferred maths problems, fact problems, evidentiary problems. His manager would attest that time management was Will's biggest problem as he never said no to work if he could find a way to fit it all in.

And yet… He found that he could not seem to roust himself to wish the woman well and get back on his way.

There was nothing to be done except to help.

Decision made, he held out both hands as if dealing with a wounded animal. "Any way you can jiggle your foot free?"

"Wow. That's a thought." It seemed she'd hit the next stage of shock—sarcasm.

"Says the woman who threw a shoe at an oncoming car in the hope of saving herself from getting squished."

Her eyes narrowed. Her fists curled tighter around her skirt. Beneath the head-to-toe finery she was pure street urchin itching for a fight.

Shock, he reminded himself. *Stuck*. And she must have been cold. There wasn't much to the top part of her dress but a few layers of lace draped over her shoulders, leaving her arms bare. The way the skirt moved as it fell to her feet made it look like layers of woven air.

Air he'd have to get a grip on if he had any hope of pulling her free.

Will slid the jacket of his morning suit from his shoulders and tossed it over the windscreen into the car. Rolling his sleeves to his elbows, he took a turn about her, eyeing the angles, finding comfort in the application of basic geometry and calculus.

She looked about five-feet-eight, give or take the foot stuck in the mud.

"What do you weigh?"

"Excuse me?"

"Never mind." It would come down to the force of the suction of the mud anyway. "If you don't mind, I'm going to take you from behind."

A slim auburn eyebrow rose dramatically. "I thank you for asking first, but I do mind."

Will's gaze lifted from the behind in question to find the woman looking over her shoulder at him. Those big eyes were unblinking, a glint of warmth, laughter even, flickering in the blue. Or was it green?

Right. He'd heard it too. He felt his own cheek curving into an unexpected smile. "My intentions are pure. I only wish to get you out of your... sticky situation."

Her right fist unclenched from her skirt, her fingers sliding past one another. Then her eyes dipped as she gave *him* a thorough once-over to match the one he'd given her.

Will crossed his arms and waited. He was the pre-eminent living name in modern astronomy. Eyes Only at NASA. An open invitation to the UN. On first-name terms with presidents and prime ministers alike.

Yet none of that mattered on this muddy country road as, with a deep sigh of unwitting capitulation, the woman waved an idle hand his way and said, "Fine. Let's get this over and done with."

First time for everything, Will thought as he moved into position. Adrenaline having been sapped away, he was now very much aware of the damage incurred by his footwear. He attempted to find purchase on the boggy ground. "Ready?"

She muttered something that sounded like, "Not even close." But then she lifted her arms.

Will wrapped his arms around her waist. There really was nothing of her. More dress than woman. He grounded his feet, and heaved.

Nothing happened. She was well-bogged.

"Grip my arms," he said. "Lean back a little. Into me."

In for a penny, she wrapped her arms over his,

her fingers shockingly cold as they curved over his wrists. But right behind the chill came that energy, like electricity humming just beneath her skin.

Will said, "On three I need you to press down strongly with your free foot, then jump. Okay?"

She nodded and another curl fell down, tumbling into his face. He blinked to dislodge a strand from his eyelashes. And a sweet, familiar scent tickled his nose till he could taste it on the back of his tongue. *Honeysuckle.*

"Here we go," he grumbled. "One. Two. And... three!"

He felt her sink into the ground and as she pushed he pulled. With a thick, wet *schlock* her foot popped free.

She spun, tottered, her feet near slipping out from under her. And finally came to a halt with her face lodged into his neck.

There she breathed. Warm bursts of air wafted over his skin and turned his hair follicles into goose flesh.

Then he felt the moment she realised she had one hand gripping his sleeve, the other clamped to his backside for all she was worth.

The breathing stopped. A heartbeat slunk by. Two. Then she slowly released her hold.

Only, the second she let go, she slipped again.

With a whoop she grabbed him—the sound shaking a pair of bluebirds loose. They swooped and twittered before chasing one another down the tunnel and away.

And suddenly she was trembling in earnest. Violent shakes racked her body, as if she were about to self-destruct.

Dammit. Computing how best to separate her from her trap was one thing, but this was beyond his pay grade.

She made a noise then. Something between a squeak and a whimper. The next time she shook she broke free with a cracking laugh. Then more laughter tumbled on top of the first. Braying, cackling, riotous laughter—the kind that took hold of a person until they could barely breathe.

Will looked to the sky. He wasn't built for this kind of roller coaster of emotion. It was so taxing and there was no logical pathway out.

Ready to take his leave before things turned again, Will took her firmly by the arms.

Another curl fell to dangle in front of her face. She crossed her eyes and blew it away with a quick stream of air shot from the side of her mouth. When she uncrossed her eyes she looked directly into his.

Spots of pretty pink sat high on her pale cheeks, clear even beneath the tracks of old tears. As her laughter faded, her wide mouth still smiled softly. Light sparked in the bluish green of her huge eyes, glints of folly and fun. And she sank into his grip as if she could stay there all day.

Instead of the words that had been balanced on the tip of his tongue, Will found himself saying, "If you're laughing because your other foot is now stuck I will leave you here."

A grin flashed across her face, fast and furious, resonant of a pulse fusion blast. "Not stuck," she said. "Muddy, mortified, falling apart at the seams, but the last thing I am any more is stuck."

Will nodded. Even though he was the one who suddenly felt stuck. For words. For a decision on what to do next. For a reason to let her go.

Which was *why* he let her go. He unclamped his fingers one at a time, giving her no reason to fall into his arms again.

The woman reminded him of a newly collapsed star, unaware as yet that her unstable gravitational field syphoned energy from everything she touched.

But Will wasn't about to give any away. He gave every bit of energy to his work. It was important, it was ground-breaking, it was necessary. He had none to spare.

"Look," he said, stopping to clear his throat. "I'm heading towards court so I can give you a lift if you're heading in that direction. Or drop you…wherever it is you are going." On foot. Through muddy countryside. In what had probably been some pretty fancy shoes, considering the party dress that went with them. From what Will had seen there was nothing for miles bar the village behind him, and the palace some distance ahead. "Were you heading to the wedding, then?"

It was a simple enough question, but the girl looked as if she'd been slapped. Laughter gone, colour gone, dark tears suddenly wobbled precariously in the corners of her eyes.

She recovered quickly, dashing a finger under each eye, sniffing and taking a careful step back. "No. No, thanks. I'm… I'll be fine. You go ahead. Thank you, though."

With that she lifted her dress, turned her back

on him and picked her way across the road, slipping a little, tripping on her skirt more.

If the woman wanted to make her own way, dressed and shod as she was, then who was he to argue? He almost convinced himself too. Then he caught the moment she glanced towards the palace, hidden somewhere on the other side of the trees, and decidedly changed tack so that she was heading in the absolute opposite direction.

And, like the snick of a well-oiled combination lock, everything suddenly clicked into place.

The dress with its layers of pink lace, voluminous skirt and hints of rose-gold thread throughout.

The pink train—was that what they called it?—trailing in the mud behind her.

Will's gaze dropped to her left hand clenched around a handful of skirt. A humungous pink rock the size of a thumbnail in a thin rose-gold band glinted thereupon.

He'd ribbed Hugo enough through school when the guy had been forced to wear the sash of his country at formal events: pink and rose-gold—the colours of the Vallemontian banner.

Only one woman in the country would be wearing a gown in those colours today.

If Will wasn't mistaken, he'd nearly run down one Mercedes Gray Leonine.

Who—instead of spending her last moments as a single woman laughing with her bridesmaids and hugging her family before heading off to marry the estimable Prince Alessandro Hugo Giordano and become a princess of Vallemont— was making a desperate, muddy, shoeless run for the hills.

Perfect.

CHAPTER TWO

"YOU CAN'T BE SERIOUS."

Sadie swallowed as the man's voice echoed through the thicket. Or she tried at the very least. After crying non-stop for the last hour, her throat felt like sandpaper.

In fact, her entire body felt raw. Sensitive. Prickly. As if her senses were turned up to eleven.

Adding a near-death experience hadn't helped a jot.

Well, pure and utter panic had got her this far and she planned to ride it out until she reached the border. Or a cave. Or a sinkhole that could swallow her up. Where was a batch of quicksand when you needed it?

She gathered as much of her dress as she was able and kept on walking, hoping her sardonic liberator would simply give up and drive away.

Unfortunately, his deep voice cut through the clearing like a foghorn. "You've made your point. You can stop walking now."

Sadie's bare foot squelched into a slippery patch of mud. She closed her eyes. Took a breath. Turned. And faced down the stranger in her midst.

When she'd heard the car coming around the corner her life had flashed before her eyes. Literally. Moments, big and small, fluttering through her mind like pages in a picture book.

Not yet school age, screaming, pigtails flying behind her as she was being chased through the palace halls by a grinning Hugo. Her mother waggling a finger at her and telling her to act like a lady.

At five, maybe six, Princess Marguerite gently reminding her not to hold her hand up to block the bright lights from the TV crew. Hugo standing behind a camera making faces as she sat on a couch in the palace library, answering questions about growing up as a "regular girl" in the palace.

The blur of high school without Hugo at her side—the first sense of feeling adrift without her safety net.

Her attempt to overcome that feeling—wide-eyed and terrified, landing in New York when she was twenty. Then grabbing that safety net

with both hands as, teary and weary, she fled
New York and moved back into the palace at
twenty-five.

Her memory had not yet hit the anxious, frac-
tured, out-of-control mess of the past few weeks
when she'd spied the driver on the muddy road.

For time had slowed—imprinting on her mind
wind-ruffled dark hair, a square jaw, a face as
handsome as sin. A surge of drama at the end.
*At least the last thing I'll ever see is a thing of
beauty*, she'd thought.

Of course, that was before he'd proceeded to
storm at her for a good five minutes straight.

Quite the voice he had. Good projection. With
those darkly scowling eyes and that muscle ticking in his impossibly firm jaw she'd first thought
him a Hamlet shoo-in. From a distance, though,
with those serious curls and proud square shoulders he'd make a fine Laertes. Then again, she'd
had a good grip on that which was hidden beneath the suit. A dashing Mercutio, perhaps?

Though not in one of her high-school produc-
tions, alas. One look at him and her twelfth-grade
drama students would be too busy swooning to
get anything done.

That, and she'd been "encouraged" to take a

sabbatical from her job the moment she'd become engaged. The palace had suggested six months for her to settle into her new role before "deciding" if she wished to return.

"Ms," he said again, and she landed back in the moment with a thud.

Focus, her subconscious demanded, lucidity fluctuating like a flickering oil lamp during a storm. Her brain seemed to have kicked into self-protect mode, preferring distraction over reality. But, as much as she might wish she was living a high-school play, this was as real as it got.

"Ms—"

"Miss," she shot back, levelling the stranger with a *leave me be* glance. Oh, yes, she was very much a "miss". Her recent actions made sure of that. She remembered the rock weighing down her left hand and carefully tucked it into a swathe of pink tulle.

"As I said I'll be fine from here. I promise. You can go." She took a decided step back, landing right on the cusp of a jagged rock. She winced. Cried out. Hopped around. Swore just a bit. Then pinched the bridge of her nose when tears threatened to spill again.

"Miss," said the stranger, his rumbling voice

quieter now, yet somehow carrying all the more. "You have lost both your shoes. You're covered in mud. You're clearly not…well. It's a mile or more to the nearest village. And the afternoon is settling in. Unless you have another mode of transport under that skirt, you're either coming with me or you're sleeping under the stars. Trust me."

Trust him? Did he think she was born under a mushroom? *Quite possibly,* she thought, considering the amount of mud covering the bottom half of her dress.

Not witness to the conversations going on inside Sadie's head, the stranger went on, "How could I look myself in the mirror if I heard on the news tomorrow that a woman was eaten by a bear, the only evidence the remains of a pink dress?"

Sadie coughed. Not a laugh. Not a whimper. More like the verbal rendering of her crumbling resolve. "Bears are rare in Vallemont. And they have plenty of fish."

"Mmm. The headline was always more likely to be *Death by Tulle.*" He swished a headline across the sky. *"'Woman trips over log hidden entirely from view by copious skirts, lands face-first in puddle. Drowns.'"*

Sadie's eye twitched. She wasn't going to smile. Not again. That earlier burst of laughter was merely the most recent mental snap on a day punctuated with mental snaps.

She breathed out hard. She'd walked miles through rain-drenched countryside in high heels and a dress that weighed as much as she did. She hadn't eaten since…when? Last night? There was a good chance she was on the verge of dehydration considering the amount of water she'd lost through her tear ducts alone. She was physically and emotionally spent.

And she needed whatever reserve of energy, chutzpah and pure guts she had left, considering what she'd be facing over the next few days, weeks, decades, when she was finally forced to face the mess she had left behind.

She gave the stranger a proper once-over. Bespoke suit. Clean fingernails. Posh accent. That certain *je ne sais quoi* that came of being born into a life of relative ease.

The fact that he had clearly not taken to her was a concern. She was likable. Extremely likable. Well known, in fact, for being universally liked. True, he'd not caught her in a banner moment, but still. Worth noting.

"You could be an axe murderer for all I know," she said. "Heck, *I* could be an axe murderer. Maybe this is my *modus operandi*."

He must have seen something in her face. Heard the subtle hitch in her voice. Either way, his head tipped sideways. Just a fraction. Enough to say, *Come on, honey. Who are you trying to kid?*

The frustrating thing was, he was right.

It was pure dumb luck that he had happened upon her right in the moment she'd become stuck. And it was dumber luck that he was a stranger who clearly had no clue who she was. For her face had been everywhere the last few weeks. Well, not *her* face. The plucked, besmeared, stylised face of a future princess. For what she had imagined would be a quiet, intimate ceremony, the legal joining of two friends in a mutually beneficial arrangement, had somehow spiralled way out of control.

She'd had more dumb luck that not a single soul had seen her climb out the window of the small antechamber at the base of the six-hundred-year-old palace chapel and run, the church bells chiming loud enough to be heard for twenty miles in every direction.

Meaning karma would be lying in wait to even out the balance.

She looked up the road. That way led to the palace. To people who'd no doubt discovered she was missing by now and would search to the ends of the earth to find her. A scattered pulse leapt in her throat.

Then she looked at the stranger's car, all rolling fenders and mag wheels, speed drawn in its every line. Honestly, if he drove a jalopy it would still get her further from trouble faster than her own feet.

Decision made, she held out a hand. "Give me your phone."

"Not an axe murderer, then, but a thief?"

"I'm going to let my mother know who to send the police after if I go missing."

"Where's your phone?"

"In my other dress."

A glint sparked deep in her accomplice's shadowed eyes. It was quite the sight, triggering a matching spark in her belly. She cleared her throat as the man bent over the car and pulled a slick black phone from a space between the bucket seats.

He waved his thumb over the screen, and when it flashed on he handed it to her.

The wallpaper on his phone was something from outer space. A shot from *Star Wars*? Maybe underneath the suave, urban hunk mystique he was a Trekkie.

The wallpaper on the phone she'd unfortunately left at the palace in her rush to get the heck out of there was a unicorn sitting at a bar drinking a "human milkshake". Best not to judge.

She found the text app, typed in her mother's number.

But what to say? *I'm sorry? I'm safe? I screwed up? I would give my right leg to make sure they do not take this out on you?*

Her mother had been a maid at the palace since before Sadie was born. It had been her home too for nearly thirty years. If they fired her mother because of what Sadie had done…

Lava-hot fear swarmed through Sadie's insides until she imagined Hugo's response to such a suggestion. No. No matter how hard he might find it to forgive her for what she'd done to him today, he'd never take it out on her mother. He was that good a man. The best man she'd ever known.

Maman

Good start.

By now you know that I'm not at the chapel.

Another deep breath.

I couldn't go through with it. It wasn't right. Not for me and certainly not for Hugo. If you see Hugo...

She paused, deleted the last line. Whatever needed to be said to Hugo, she would say herself.

I'm so terribly, desperately sorry for all the confusion and complications that will come of this and I promise I will make everything right. But today, right now, I have to lick my wounds, clear my head and prepare. Know that until then that I'm whole and I'm safe. xXx

Before she could change her mind, she pressed "send". Only remembering belatedly that her mother wouldn't recognise the strange phone number.

In fact...

She found the camera app, held up the phone

and said, "Smile!" Her benefactor turned and she took a photo.

She quickly started a new message. Added the picture.

I've borrowed this phone from the gentleman in this picture, so do not message back. I'll call when I can. Love you.

The picture slid up the screen as the message was sent. The top of his head was missing, and an ear, but it was still him in all his grumpy glory. His hand was at his tie, giving it a tormented tug. His dark eyes bored into the lens. He wasn't smiling but there was something about the shape of his mouth, a curving at the corners, the barest hint of what might—under just the right circumstances—become a dimple.

Her thumb hovered over the screen as she thought about sending a text to Hugo too. What if the poor lady-in-waiting she'd sent off into the palace with the note to Hugo clutched in her white-knuckled grip hadn't managed to get through to him? Even if she had, Sadie still needed to tell him…to explain…

What? That she was nothing but a scaredy-cat?

She slid her thumbs away from the screen.

"Done?" the phone owner asked.

Sadie deleted the conversation. She hoped her mother would heed her warning or her cover as a possible axe murderess would be blown.

She solemnly gave him back his phone. "And now I'll go in your car with you."

"You're a brave woman."

"You have no idea."

His mouthed twitched and…there. Dimple. Heaven help the women of the world who got to see that thing in full flight.

Not *her* though.

If her mother had taught her anything it was to beware instant appeal; it had everything to do with genetic luck and nothing to do with character. A handsome smile could be fleeting, and could be used to hide all manner of sins.

With that in mind, it had taken her twenty-nine years to agree to marry Hugo and he'd been her best friend since birth. And still, when it had come to the crunch, she'd run. Something she'd learned from her father.

Sadie felt the backs of her eyes begin to burn as the home truths settled in. But she was done crying. She mentally forced the tears away.

She'd made a choice today. One that had sent her down this road alone. And alone she had to remain if she was to get her head on straight and figure out what the heck she was going to do with the rest of her life. But Grouchy Dimples wasn't going to leave her alone unless she let him do his knight-in-shining-armour bit and get her safely out of sight.

So Sadie picked her way back through the rivulets of rock and dirt and mud.

The stranger moved around to the passenger side of the car, opened the door, bowed slightly and said, "My lady."

Sadie's entire body froze. Only her eyes moved to collide with his.

She looked for a gleam of knowledge, a sign that he knew exactly who she was. But the only sign she got was the return of the tic in his jaw. He couldn't wait to get rid of her either.

"Sadie," she said before she even felt the word forming. "My name, it's…just Sadie."

"Pleasure to meet you, Just Sadie. I'm Will."

He held out a hand. She took it. He felt warm where she was cool. Strong where she was soft. His big hand enveloped hers completely, and for the first time in as long as she could remember she found herself hit with the profound sense that everything was going to be okay.

The sensation was so strong, so unexpected, so unsought, she whipped her hand away.

Will held the door for her once more. "Let's get this show on the road."

Taking a deep breath, Sadie gathered up as much of her skirt as she could, tucking and folding and looping the fabric under her arms. Then she squeezed backside-first into the bucket seat.

After Will closed the door with a soft snick, Sadie let the fabric go. It sprung away, filling the space right up to her chin. Relief at not being on her feet, on the run, in the open, rolling over her like a wave of bliss.

Will slid into the driver's seat and curled long fingers over the leather steering wheel. He surreptitiously checked his watch again. He still thought he had a wedding to attend, Sadie realised, and for a fraught second she thought he might simply drive that way.

"You mentioned a village," Sadie said, pointing over her shoulder in the opposite direction to the palace.

"The village it is." Will gunned the engine, carefully backed out of the muddy trench, executed a neat three-point turn and drove back the way he had come.

A minute later, Sadie glimpsed the palace through the trees. The afternoon sunlight had begun to cast the famous pink and gold highlights across the sandstone walls which had lent the small principality the beautiful, romantic, quixotic colours of its banners.

Home.

But after what she had done, could she ever go back there? Would they even let her through the door? And what would happen to her mother, a maid who had lived and worked under the palace roof for the last twenty-nine years?

Sadie put the flurry of unpleasant questions to one side and closed her eyes, letting the dappled sunlight wash across the backs of her eyelids. There was nothing she could do about all that right now.

Later. She'd figure it all out later.

Will leant his elbow against the window of the car, feigning a relaxedness he did not feel as he drove over the bridge he'd navigated not long before. Back in the village, banners still flew. Music poured out into the streets. The roads were now bare, since everyone had moved inside to be in front of their TVs in order to see the bride make her first appearance. Little did they know they were looking the wrong way.

If Hugo hadn't yet discovered his bride was missing, he soon would. Search plans would be afoot. Containment plans.

Will was forced to admit that his immediate plans would need to become fluid for the moment as well. But first…

As the engine's throaty growl gave him away, Sadie sat upright. "What are you doing? Why are you slowing?"

"We need petrol," he said as he pulled off the road and up to a tank wrapped in rose-gold tinsel that flapped in the light breeze.

He used the collective noun very much on purpose. He'd read enough books to know that, in hostage negotiations, making the hostage-taker feel they were on the same side was paramount. Though which one of them was the hostage here was debatable.

He pulled over and jumped from the car. But not before surreptitiously sliding his phone into his pocket.

Meanwhile, Sadie had slunk down so far in the

seat she was practically in the footwell. All he could see was acres of crinkled pink and a few auburn curls.

"Can you breathe down there?"

A muffled voice professed, "Most of the dress is organically grown Australian cotton. Very breathable."

"And yet I'm not sure it was intended to be worn over the face."

Two hands curled around the fabric and a small face poked out. "Point made."

She blinked at him through huge red-rimmed eyes above a pink-tipped nose. Her full lower lip was shiny from nibbling. When she wasn't acting so bolshie and stubborn she was rather pretty.

Will pushed the thought away. He turned his back and splashed a nominal amount of petrol into the tank before heading for the shop. Inside, he gave the guy behind the counter a wave. Then, finding a private corner, he made the call, using a phone number he could only hope still worked.

It answered on the second ring.

"Yes?" came the voice from Will's past. The voice of the Prince.

Will leaned against a shelf. "Hey, mate, how's things?"

A beat. "Darcy? Look, I can't—"

"You can't talk because you're meant to be getting married but your bride seems to have gone missing."

The silence was deafening. Then footsteps echoed through the phone as Hugo obviously set to finding himself a private corner of his own.

"How the hell can you possibly—?"

"She's with me."

Will gave a very quick rundown of the events. Leading to his decision to keep her close.

Hugo's voice was uncommonly hoarse, even a little cracked, as he said, "I was given a note just before you rang by a maid refusing to leave my doorway. Written in lipstick, on the torn-out page of a hymnal no less, telling me she couldn't go through with it. I didn't believe it until just now. Yet at the same time it felt like I'd been waiting for that note all my life. I— *Dammit*. Excuse me a moment."

Hugo's voice was muffled. Will imagined him covering the mouthpiece of the phone. His tension was palpable in his short, sharp responses to whomever had disrupted their conversation.

It had been years since he'd seen Hugo in person. Even as a teenager there'd been gravitas about the Prince, the weight of the world sitting easily on his shoulders. Until his own father had died in a car crash and that world had collapsed.

Will had born Hugo through that horrendous time. Hugo had tried to return the favour after Clair's death only a few months later, putting aside his own grief, but Will had rejected Hugo's counsel out of hand.

Will had been mistaken then. He would not turn his back on the Prince now.

Will waited, glancing around the petrol station. Pink and gold streamers hung limply from the ceiling to the cash register. The guy behind the counter hunched over a small TV while sipping pink milk through a straw. The vision showed a variety of invited guests smiling and waving as they walked up the gravel path to the palace gates.

A frisson of tension pulled tight across Will's shoulders. Everything had happened so fast—the near crash, the rescue, the discovery, the uncommon decision to get involved—the repercussions that went far beyond his inconvenience didn't hit him until that moment.

An entire country held its breath in anticipation, clueless as to the axe that had already begun to swing, while Hugo sat somewhere in the palace, looking into the face of an emotional ruination that he did not deserve. Again.

"Apologies," said Hugo as he came back on the line.

"Mate," said Will, his own voice a little rough. "What the hell happened?"

The silence was thick. Distant. Elongating the miles and years between them.

Hugo's voice was cool as he asked, "Is she injured? Is she distressed?"

"She's shaky but unhurt."

"I'd very much like to talk to her."

Will thought *he'd* very much like to kick her out of his rental car, and dump her on the side of the road; force her to face the bedlam she had unleashed. But it was clear Hugo was not of the same mind.

If Will's intention in coming to Vallemont had truly been to put things to rights with his oldest friend, then it seemed he'd been gifted the opportunity to do just that. The fact it would not be easy was ironically just.

"In full disclosure, she doesn't know I'm talking to you. In fact, she doesn't know that I'm aware of who she is at all. I believe that's the only reason she agreed to let me give her a lift."

He let that sit. When Hugo made no demur, Will went on.

"I can give her the phone or I can keep her with me until you send someone to collect her. Unless, of course, you want me to bring her back right now so you can work your magic and marry the girl."

He half hoped Hugo would say *Bring back my girl*—then Will could deliver her and tell himself he'd achieved what he'd come to Vallemont to do.

"If you could stay with her I would very much appreciate it," was Hugo's eventual response. "I'll send for her when I can. Till then, keep her safe."

Will nodded before saying, "Of course. And you? Where do you go from here?"

"That, my friend, would be the question of the hour."

"As opposed to, *Do you take this woman?*" Will imagined a wry smile filling the silence. And suddenly the miles and years contracted to nothing.

"Yes," was Hugo's dry response. "As opposed to that."

The Prince rang off first. No doubt plenty on his to-do list.

It left Will to stare at the picture he'd linked to Hugo's private line; the two of them at seventeen in climbing gear, grins wide, arms slung around one another's shoulders, mountains at their backs. Clair had taken that picture the day before Will had broken his leg.

By the end of that summer Clair had been taken ill. A week later she'd been diagnosed with an incurable brain disease. Mere months after she'd taken that photo she'd left them for ever.

Will slid his phone into his pocket. He tucked the memories away too before they started to feed on him rather than the other way around.

Hugo wasn't the only one with things to do.

Only, while Hugo would no doubt be fending off a buffet of advisors as he determined the best way forward, Will had to go it alone.

It was a concept that didn't come easily to a twin, a concept that had haunted him for a long time after his sister was gone. Until one day, while hiding from his economics professor at Cambridge, he'd slipped into a random lecture hall. Taken a seat at the back. Discovered it was

Stars and the Cosmic Cycle. And found himself skewered to the seat.

For Clair's last gift to him, one she'd planned to give to him on what would have been their eighteenth birthday, one he'd only found in her bedroom after she'd died, was a telescope.

As a man who'd never believed in signs, he'd gone with it. As the lecturer had talked of the universe as unmapped, unchartered and mostly incalculable, many in the lecture hall had twittered and shifted on their seats, finding the concept overwhelming.

For Will it had changed the concept of being "alone" for him completely. And it was that ability to dissociate from the everyday, to enjoy a high level of dedicated solitude, that had paved the way for his being the pre-eminent voice in modern astronomy.

Will paid for the petrol, steadfastly refusing to look at the pre-wedding coverage on the monitor. He was halfway to the car when he remembered.

He wasn't alone.

He had Sadie.

She peered up at him from the mound of wriggling pink as he slid back into the car, her curls flopping onto her pale shoulders, her big eyes filled with pandemonium. This woman was chaos incarnate, and she was leaving a widening swathe of trouble in her wake.

"Everything okay?" she asked. "You were gone for a while."

"Was I?" Will started the car with more gusto than required.

He'd come to this country, pained at the thought of having to watch Hugo marry someone who wasn't Clair, quietly wondering if the invitation was his penance for having laid the blame for what had happened at Hugo's guiltless feet for all these years.

Now he realised he'd miscalculated. *She* was his penance. Mercedes "Sadie" Gray Leonine. Looking after her on Hugo's behalf, keeping her out of sight until he could send word to Hugo where he could find her would go some way to ameliorating past wrongs.

And when it was done, he might even be able to get an earlier flight out. It was meant to be an unusually clear night, a rare opportunity to spend some time with London's night sky.

Feeling better about the world, Will shot Sadie a smile, which faded a tad at the way her eyes widened as he did so.

"The tank is full, the sky is blue." Will tapped the car's GPS. "North? South? East? West? Coast? Mountains? Moon? Where are we going?"

CHAPTER THREE

SADIE NIBBLED SO hard on the tip of a pale pink acrylic nail, the thing snapped right off, so she carefully hid it in the door pocket and racked her brain for an answer.

Where are we going? Will had asked. As if she were following some kind of plan.

Her only goal had been to get as far from the palace as possible without being seen. Her luck would not hold out for much longer. Her best bet now was to hole up, get in touch with Hugo somehow. Apologise, grovel, make him see that while her timing had been terrible it had been the right decision, for both of them.

"A room," she said. "To stay for a night. That's what I'd like."

"Excellent. Do you have a place in mind?"

"Not exactly. Some place…quiet would be fine." Discreet. Not one of Hugo's palatial resorts, for example. "Where are those dodgy motels you see in American cop shows when you need them?"

"I'm sorry?"

Sadie glanced at her companion, thankful to find he was back to looking at her as if he was barely containing his impatience. That momentary flash of perfect white teeth as he'd smiled had been disconcerting to say the least.

She usually went out of her way to make people feel comfortable. Hugo joked that her need to be liked by everyone was pathological. Sadie simply wanted to make sure everyone around her was happy. But in these circumstances a little distance felt safer. It was easier to think of the man as a means to an end rather than a collection of dimples, warm hands and crinkles at the edges of his eyes as he smiled. Especially now, when she was feeling so untethered. In the past her decision-making skills had not been at their peak at such times.

She turned on the seat; her skirt bunching under her hip. "You know, the kind where the anti-hero in the vintage brown Cadillac hooks around the back of some dreary, anonymous, flat-roofed roadside joint where the ancient woman with a cigarette dangling from her cracked lips doesn't even bother to look up from her cross-word as she signs the guy in?"

He glanced at her and said, "Flat-roofed?"

How odd that he focused on that. It was the kind of detail that usually tickled only her. When she found herself looking into those dark eyes of his a beat too long, she glanced at her fake fingernails instead. One down, nine to go. "You know—squat. Like it's been flattened by the weight of the world. Why doesn't Vallemont have places like that?"

"Because it's Vallemont," he said, and he was right.

The sentiment wouldn't have made as much sense to her as a kid.

Watching Hugo go away to school had made Sadie itch to see the world, to see life outside the borders of the peaceable country in which she'd been born. And eventually she'd managed to talk her way into a four-year acting course in New York.

At first it had been a dream. Auditioning, waitressing, living in near-squalor with three strangers in a studio in Brooklyn. Walking streets where nobody knew her story, with its urban canyons, subway smells, its cracked sidewalks and manic energy, as different a place from Vallemont as it was possible to find.

Halfway through she'd begun to feel lonely, the brilliant, fraught, nerve-racking, ugly, beautiful and eye-opening experience taking its toll.

By the end of that year she'd realised that it wasn't the noise and hustle and energy of a big city she had craved, but control over her life. Taking control over her narrative. That's what she loved about theatre. Not acting, but the chance to shape a play from beginning to end.

She'd lasted another year before she'd come home. Giving up a dream many would kill for.

And oh, that land of rolling hills and green pastures. Of crystalline streams fed by snow-capped mountains. And towns of cobbled streets and dappled sunshine and quiet, happy lives. The relief had been immeasurable.

And here she was again—gifted a rare opportunity and she'd thrown it all away.

Sadie groaned and let her head drop back against the seat.

"If it's accommodation you're after, what about this place?" said Will, the car engine growling as he slowed.

Sadie cracked open an eye to find herself looking at a place as far from a dreary, anonymous, flat-roofed roadside joint as possible.

A sign reading "La Tulipe" swung from the eaves of a ramshackle dwelling, three storeys high, with a pitched roof and balconies all round. Bright purple bougainvillaea was starkly stunning as it crept over the muddy brick. Oddly shaped, it dissected two roads, one heading up the hill to the left, the other dipping down the hill sharply to the right, creating an optical illusion that made it look as if it had a slight lean down the hill. Or maybe it *was* falling down the hill. It had an ancient, ramshackle appeal either way.

A skinny black cat skittered across the way as Will pulled into a spot on the low side of the building. He turned off the engine, got out of the car and reached into the back seat for a soft black leather bag.

Sadie sat up straight. "Ah, what are you doing with those?"

"I plan on seeing you inside. And I'm not leaving my bags in the car while I do so."

Sadie peeked over her shoulder. A gentle breeze skipped autumn leaves over the cobbled road. A small brown bird danced from one semi-bare tree to another. Other than that, there was no one as far as the eye could see. "We're not exactly a crime capital here."

Will followed her gaze, paused a moment, then, ignoring her, heaved his other bag—a big square silver case—out of the car and set it on the footpath. "Coming?"

Sadie heard voices—a couple laughing as they crossed the street at the bottom of the hill. Time to get inside. Except…

"I can't go in there dressed like this. I look—" Like the girl who'd left the country's most eligible bachelor standing at the altar. She'd be less likely to be recognised naked than in that dress. She'd heard knock-offs were already available. "A total mess. What do you have in your bag? Or your case?"

Will's hand went to the battered silver case. It was big enough that she might even fit inside. For a brief moment she considered asking.

"Anything I might be able to borrow? I'll take it off the minute I get inside a room."

That muscle ticked in his jaw. Another flickered below his right eye. He appeared to be making a great effort at keeping eye contact. And Sadie realised what she'd said.

Feeling a wave of pink heat rising up her neck,

she backtracked. "I mean I'll find something else to wear, even if it's a bed sheet, then you can be on your way."

Her reluctant knight breathed for a beat or two, his dark eyes pinning her to her seat. Then, muttering under his breath, he lifted the leather bag and plonked it onto the driver's seat.

Then he moved down the footpath and away from the car, his back to her, giving her some privacy. Not ideal, but needs must.

Inside his bag she found an expensive-looking knit sweater. Black. Soft as a baby's bottom. It smelled delicious too. Like sandalwood, and fresh air and man. Like the scent she'd caught in that strangely intimate half a second where Will had put his arms around her, pulling her back into the nook of his strong, warm body, before yanking her out of the mud.

She cleared her throat and shoved the sweater aside, rifling until she found a utilitarian tracksuit top. Black again. And some black tracksuit pants. The guy sure liked black. Maybe he was a spy. Or a magician. Or clinically depressed.

She glanced over her shoulder to find he still had his back to her as he stood on the footpath, hands in pockets, face tilted to the sun.

Even in a suit it was clear he was built like a champion diver—all broad shoulders and thick, roping muscle. His profile as he squinted down the street was strong, sure, forbearing. He might not be the most easy-going man she'd ever met, but there was no doubting he was very comfortable in his own skin.

Not depressed, then. Perhaps he simply liked black.

She pulled out the tracksuit pants, shuffled up onto her knees, twisted her hands over her shoulder to attempt to rid herself of layers of lace embedded with tiny pink crystals…no luck. She twisted around the back of her waist. Still no luck. As panic tickled up her spine she thought about ripping the thing over her head, but it was so dense she'd probably find herself caught in a straightjacket of her own making.

Sadie bit her lip and looked up at the sky. Cloudless. The brightest blue. Such a happy sight. She muttered a few choice words under her breath.

Then, "Ah, excuse me. Will? I need some help here."

He spun on his heel so the sun was behind him, his face in shadow. Resistance was evident in the hard lines of his body as he said, "Help?"

She flapped her hand towards the trillion pearl buttons strapping her in.

It was his turn to mutter a flurry of choice words before he took a few slow steps her way. "What do you need me to do?"

"Start at the top? Truth be told, I wasn't paying much attention as I was strapped in." Trying not to panic had been higher on her list of priorities.

Will took in a long, deep breath before his hands moved to her neck, surprisingly gentle as they pushed her hair aside. So many curls had dropped during her run from the palace. She helped, taking them in hand as she tipped her head forward.

A beat later, Will's fingers worked the top button, which was positioned right against a vertebra. That was what it felt like anyway, as if he'd hit a nerve cluster. Goosebumps sprung up all over her body.

With a sweet glide, it unhooked, Will's warm thumb sliding against her skin as he pressed the fabric aside.

"Sadie?" he asked, his voice deep and low and close enough to cause a rumble.

"Yes, Will?"

"There are about a hundred-odd buttons on this thing."

"One hundred and eight." One for every year the Giordanos had been the governing family of Vallemont. Seriously. When the small wedding she and Hugo had planned had twisted into the kind of circus where the number of pearl buttons on her dress had a backstory, that was when she ought to have put her foot down and called the whole thing off.

Will said, "Take this as a serious question, but are there…layers underneath the dress?"

"Layers?"

"Ah, under…garments?"

She'd not been able to pin down his accent until that moment. It was crisp and clear, but worldly. As if he'd travelled a great deal. In that moment it was pure, upper-crust, Queen's English.

He sounded so adorably repressed, she was unable to stop herself from saying, "Are you asking if I've gone commando?"

A beat, a breath. Then, "Sure. Why not?"

"No, Will. I am not naked beneath my dress. There are undergarments to spare."

"Glad to hear it. And are you planning on wearing your dress again?"

"Once this thing is off I never want to see it again, much less wear it!" A tad effusive perhaps?

"Excellent. Here goes." Solid nails scraped lightly against her shoulder muscles as his fingers dived beneath the fabric. Then with a rip that split the silence he tore the dress apart. Buttons scattered with a pop-pop-pop as they hit the dashboard, the steering wheel, the metal skin of the car.

As the fabric loosened and fell forward across her chest, Sadie heaved in a big, gasping breath. The first proper lungful of air she'd managed in hours. Days even. Weeks maybe. It might well have been the first true breath she'd taken since she and Hugo had shaken hands on an agreement to wed.

She felt the moment Will let the fabric go, the weight of his warm hands lifting away. More goosebumps popped up to fill the gaps between the others.

"Thank you," she said, her voice a little rough, as she wriggled free of the thing until she was in her bra, chemise and stockings.

Out of the corner of her eye she saw Will turn

away again, this time to lean his back against the car.

As the chill autumn air nipped at her skin she hastened Will's clothes over the top. There was that scent again. This time she also caught layers of leather and skin and cologne. Subtle, expensive and drinkable. The sooner she was out of his clothes the better.

Kicking her dress into the footwell with more force than was probably necessary, Sadie got out of the car.

The stony ground was freezing against her bare toes. Bracing.

When Will's tracksuit pants—which were far too big for her—began to fall, she twisted the waistband and shoved it into the top of her knickers. The jacket falling halfway down her thighs covered the lump.

At last, she bent to check herself in the side mirror. And literally reared back in shock at the sight. Her hair was an absolute disaster. Her cheeks were blotchy and wind-chafed. She could barely recognise herself beneath the rivers of dried mascara bleeding down her cheeks.

Licking her thumbs, she wiped her face clean as best she could. Then she set to pulling out the thousand pins from her hair. Dislodging the hair-piece was a blessed relief.

Once her hair was all her own again she tipped over her head, ran fingers through the knots, and massaged life back into her skull. With practised fingers, she tied the lot into a basic ponytail. No longer a clown bride. Now she was rocking more of an athletic goth look.

An athletic Goth with a mighty big engagement ring on her finger.

She glanced Will's way. He was checking some-thing on his silver case.

She looked back to the ring. It was insanely os-tentatious, with its gleaming pink diamond ba-guette in the rose-gold band. But was it her? Not even close.

Hugo's face slid into her mind then, with his oh-so-familiar laugh.

"My grandmother left it to me, which was a matter of contention in the family, as you can imagine. Her intention was that I give it to my bride. I'm sorry."

"Sorry for what?"

"It looks ridiculous on you."

"Thanks a lot!"

"Seriously. Your fingers are so scrawny, it

looks like you're trying to balance a brick on the back of your hand. Take it off."

"No. Never. Do you remember the first time you said you'd marry me? I do. I was four and you were seven. Kind woman that I am, I never planned to hold you to it back then. But I'm not letting you off the hook now. This ring is what it is: a symbol. If a brick is what will help keep roofs over both of our families' heads, then it seems like a pretty fine symbol to me."

Another promise broken, Sadie slid the brick from her finger. The fact that it came right off, without even the slightest pressure, seemed like a pretty big sign in and of itself.

She quickly tugged down the track pants, found a ribbon hanging from her garter and tied the ring to it with a nice tight knot. Then she gave the jacket one last tug. "Okay, I'm ready."

Will pressed away from the car and turned. His dark gaze danced over her clothes—*his* clothes— her bare feet, then up to her hair. It paused there a moment before dropping to the hand clutching the bouffant of fake curls. At which point his mouth kicked into a smile. Dimple and all.

As it had been the first time, it was as unexpected and magnificent as a ray of sun slicing through a rain cloud and Sadie's heart thumped against her chest.

"What?" she shot back.

Will held a hand towards the doorway of La Tulipe. "I didn't say a thing."

Sadie grabbed the hood of his jacket and pulled it over her head. Then, scooting past him, her chin imperiously high, she said, "You didn't have to."

As soon as they entered the lobby of the old hotel, Sadie's adrenaline kicked up a notch. For all her efforts to escape, everything could fall apart right here, right now.

She tucked herself in behind Will, breathing through her mouth so as not to drink too deeply of the deliciousness of his cologne. Skin. Washing detergent. Whatever.

"Sadie," he said, turning so she was face to face with his strong profile. The heavy brow, nose so perfect it could have been carved from marble, the hint of that dimple.

"Mmm?"

"Have you heard of a little something called personal space?"

"Sorry," she said, searching desperately for a

sane reason why she might be snuggled into him as she was. "I'm…cold."

If Will didn't believe her, he didn't say so. No doubt he already thought her a lunatic, considering her behaviour thus far.

As they approached the desk, over Will's shoulder Sadie saw a girl in her late teens wearing jeans and a plain pink T-shirt, her long brown hair in a side ponytail.

Will came to a stop, tipping his big silver case back onto its wheels and readjusting his leather bag on his shoulder.

The girl smiled as they approached. "Hello!" she sing-songed. Then she seemed to notice Will anew, as along with a little sigh came a breathy, "Oh, my. Oh… Ah. Didn't think we'd see a soul today. The entire country has its nose up against its collective TVs. Waiting for the wedding to begin!"

She motioned to her computer monitor and Sadie was bombarded with a montage of images—crowds lining the path leading to the palace waving Vallemontian flags and throwing pink peony petals into the street. The front doors of the St Barnabas Chapel were open, inviting, a mouth waiting to swallow a bride whole.

"Prince Alessandro is so dreamy," said the girl, "don't you think? Those eyes. That voice. He's like the hero from some novel. To think, there is a woman out there who gets to be his heroine."

Sadie let her head fall, gently landing on one of Will's shoulder blades. "A room," she stage-whispered. "Ask about a room."

Will cleared his throat. "We were hoping for a room."

The girl blinked, seemed to suddenly notice Sadie hiding behind Will's shoulder.

Having been seen, Sadie fixed the hood tighter over her head, then gave the girl a little wave. She held her breath, waiting for the moment of recognition. But the girl merely gave her a nod before her gaze slid right back to Will.

"Right. Well, lucky for you the Tower Room has just come free. The couple using it had a wicked fight. She stormed out. He followed, looking most chagrined. It was all very exciting. Like Beatrice and Benedick in person."

Sadie perked up. The girl was into *Much Ado About Nothing*? It was Sadie's absolute favourite play. She taught it to her senior students every year. Perhaps this place was a good choice after all.

"Anyway," said the girl, "it's our finest room.

Canopy bed. Kitchenette. Balcony with views that extend all the way to the palace."

Sadie's perk was short-lived. Views of the palace? No! *No, no, no...*

She must have said it out loud, as Will leaned back an inch. "No?"

Sadie bit her lip.

"Oh. Well, I'm afraid that's the only room we have. And you're not likely to find another this close to the palace. We've been booked out for weeks. Ever since the date of the royal wedding was announced. Prince Alessandro is a favourite. Many a heart broke the moment the news came through that he was to settle down for good."

"Did they, now?" Will asked, with something akin to humour edging his voice. A catch. An aside. Like an inside joke. Or was she imagining it? "The Tower Room sounds just perfect? Thank you."

A beat slunk by, followed by another, after which Sadie realised Will was waiting for her. As this was the point at which she was meant to give her details. And her money.

She lifted herself a little higher, high enough she could mutter near Will's ear, "I don't exactly have my wallet on me right now."

"In your other dress?" he muttered back.

"Uh-huh."

His hand slid between them, grazing her belly through his tracksuit top. She gasped, her breath shooting past his ear.

He turned to stone. "Sadie," he said, his voice seeming even lower than normal.

"Mmm-hmm?"

"Wallet's in my back pocket," he said.

"Right. Sorry."

Sadie rocked back onto her heels, giving Will room. When he slid a shiny black card from inside, Sadie wasn't exactly trying to catch his name...not really. But catch it she did.

Dr William Darcy.

Dr Darcy, eh? Doctor of what? William suited him more than Will. Will was a friendly name. Will Darcy—

It was Sadie's turn to turn to stone.

Surely Mr Tall Dark and Grouchy wasn't *the* Will Darcy—schoolfriend of Hugo's from his murky boarding-school days and the only person Hugo had insisted they invite to their wedding back when the plan had been to keep it small?

Her gaze danced over the back of the man's

head and neck, as if hoping for clues. But alas his collar gave nothing away.

All the while, Will's finger pressed down hard on the card and stopped its counter-slide. "Dare I ask what might the room rate be at this late date?"

The girl looked at Will, looked at his shiny card, then with a bright smile quoted an exorbitant nightly price more suited to a famous Fifth Avenue penthouse than a crumbling old village building. "Blame the wedding."

"Oh, I do," Will grumbled as he slowly lifted his finger from the card.

And Sadie felt the ground tip out from under her.

It *was* him. It had to be.

It was him and he knew. He knew who she was, he knew what she'd done. It all made sense! His coolness towards her, his insistence she go with him, the fact he was being so obliging, despite the fact he ought to have been fretting about getting to the wedding late.

The cad had been lying to her about who he was the entire time!

Okay, fine. She was lying too. But her reasons were *life and death*. Or near enough. In the olden days she would have been stoned for the move she'd pulled.

His motivation could not possibly be so clean.

"Lovely," said the girl after swiping and checking Will's card. "All set. Here are your keys."

What was that? Keys? Plural? Hang on a second. Sadie opened her mouth to let the girl know she only needed one, but Will had already picked them up.

"I'm Janine," said the girl as she came around the desk. "If you need anything, anything at all, I'm your girl. Until then, head up both sets of stairs; your door is the last on the right. I trust you'll find it wonderfully comfortable. The Tower Room also has its own fireplace. Fur rugs throughout. Super-comfortable sofas. And the most gorgeous bed you will ever see. There's no TV, of course, because it's our honeymoon suite."

Of course it is, thought Sadie, right at the moment Will said the exact same words.

A bubble of crazed laughter escaped her throat, though it sounded more like a whimper.

"Have a lovely stay, Dr Darcy and...friend."

"Thank you, Janine," he said, tapping his forehead in a two-finger salute and earning himself another sigh.

Then he turned to face Sadie. "Ready?"

Sadie gave him the same salute.

When his mouth twitched, that dimple showed for one brief second. Sadie ducked her chin and took off for the stairs.

The Tower Room was as advertised.

Exposed brick walls covered in romantic prints by Waterhouse and Rossetti. Polished wood floors gleamed in the fading light of day. Soft couches looked as if you'd fall in and never want to get out. A fireplace big enough to sleep in.

It was charming, inviting and terribly romantic.

Only then did she see the bed.

For there it was, perched on a slightly raised platform at the end of the room. Soft, cream-coloured blankets covered the mattress. Pretty gold gauze trailed from a canopy, falling into pools on the floor at each corner while fake ivy twisted around its beams and posts.

It looked like something a fairy-tale princess would sleep in.

Panic welling within her once more, Sadie looked for an out. Stumbling to one side of the room, which from the outside mirrored a classic castle keep, she pushed open the French windows and stepped onto the tiny, round balcony.

Gripping the cold metal, she gulped in great lungs full of crisp, late autumn air, hoping not to be sick all over Will's clothes.

When she finally got her stomach under control she opened her eyes.

Janine was right. The view was breathtaking.

The village lay before her, all warm, tumbling brick and thatched roofs. Early lamplight laced together rambling cobbled paths. Flower pots, green corners and naked-branched trees were scattered prettily about.

And then she looked up.

The glorious jagged mountains that surrounded their landlocked little corner of the world thrust up into the sky. And right smack dab in the middle of the view, like a gem in the centre of a ring, sat the Palace of Vallemont.

Pink ceremonial flags flapped in the breeze, all across the rooftops, heralding the big occasion. And then, as if someone had simply been waiting for her to watch, the flag atop the highest tower slid slowly down the flagpole.

If the raising of the flag signified glory, honour, rejoicing, the lowering was a sign of a death in the family, a tragedy in the country, a moment of great national sorrow.

The news was out.

Soon everybody would know she had run.

Talk about breathtaking.

CHAPTER FOUR

SADIE BACKED SLOWLY into the room, feeling as if her insides had been scooped out.

When she'd come home from New York she'd felt like such a disappointment. She'd let down everyone who'd rooted for her. Having to tell the story of her withered dream over and over again had been an out-of-body experience.

This was way worse. Millions of people she'd never met would be reeling with dismay.

Sadie was not used to being disliked. In fact, her likeability was the cornerstone of her identity.

Her story was well-known all across Vallemont, she having been born literally on the road to the palace.

Her father—a less than exemplary model of manhood who had been dragging his pregnant girlfriend across the country to avoid debt collectors—had taken one look at newborn Sadie and fled. Luckily, the wife of the reigning Sovereign Prince—Hugo's Aunt Marguerite—had been driving past when she found them, huddled on a patch of grass. The Princess had famously taken them in and given Sadie's mother a job as a palace maid, allowing Sadie to grow up as a palace child. Sadie had been a firm favourite ever since.

The very thought of all that hatred coming her way drained the blood from her extremities until she could no longer feel her toes.

Someone cleared their throat.

Sadie's focus shifted until she saw her reluctant rescuer, the living embodiment of unfavourable judgment, standing in the centre of the room holding his bags.

The only person she could possibly turn to, the only person she could lean on, ask for advice, was looking at her with all the warmth of a shadow. His dark energy added layers to her discomfort, making her feel edgy. Awkward. Hyper-aware.

Okay, she thought. This situation seems overwhelming, impossible even. But all you can expect yourself to do is handle one thing at a time. Starting with the thing right in front of you.

Dr Will Darcy.

He was the right age to have gone to school

with Hugo. That elevated level of self-confidence was certainly comparable. Though where Hugo oozed sophistication and class as if he'd been dipped in them at birth, Will had the personality of a wounded bear: gruff, unpredictable. Dangerous.

She nibbled on one of her remaining fake nails.

In the end it didn't matter. What mattered was thanking him and sending him on his way.

She moved to the small table behind the couch and grabbed some La Tulipe stationery and a pen. "Will. Thank you. So much. Truly. You've gone above and beyond. If you leave your contact details I'll know where to send the money to pay you back. Petrol, car cleaning, laundry, the hotel bill. Whatever expenses you've incurred."

He slowly shook his head. "Not necessary."

Sadie flapped the stationery his way. "But it is. Necessary. I don't like being beholden to anybody."

"Really."

Wow. Passive-aggressive, much? Sadie's shoulders snapped together, annoyance rising in her belly. He *really* didn't like her and wasn't even trying to hide it. Well, he was no prince either.

Sadie held back the desire to tell him so. Barely. Years of practice at being nice coming to the fore.

"Okay, then. I officially relieve you of your knight-in-shining-armour duties." Sadie waved her fingers as if she were sprinkling fairy dust in his general direction.

Will's expression changed. It was a miniscule shift. Barely akin to an intake of breath. But she felt it. Like a ripple of energy beneath the gruff exterior. *Game on.*

He hefted the smaller bag onto the couch. Then he nudged his muddy shoes off his feet in the way men did—using the toes to shove them past the heels. He picked them up, dropped them at the door, then padded into the small kitchenette.

"I'm thirsty. You?" he asked.

With an exaggerated yawn, she said, "I am exhausted though. I think the first thing I'll do after you have your drink and go is take a nice long nap."

Will took his time filling a glass with water from the tap. Then he turned, leaning against the bench. His voice a rumble across the room. "I'm not going anywhere just yet."

A strange little flicker of heat leapt in her belly before she smacked it down. *That* wasn't what he meant. Even if it was, now was not the time, or place…

The corner of his mouth lifted, as if he knew exactly what she was thinking. It was unnerving. *He* was unnerving. She'd been so sure he didn't like her. But maybe she had it all backwards and—

Then he said, "My tracksuit. I'd like it back."

Right. Of course! He was waiting to get his clothes back. What was wrong with her?

She was a mess, that was what was wrong. Scared, disoriented and emotionally wrecked. Not at all herself. She felt a small amount of relief at the realisation that that was why every little thing Will did—his every look, every word, every dig—was getting under her skin.

She managed a laugh. "Right. Sorry! What a goof. I'll just…find an alternative. Get you your clothes and then you can be on your way."

He took another sip of water and gave her nothing in response.

She spun around. Near the bed was a pair of doors. Behind one was a bathroom. Ooh, how lovely! A bath the size of a small car. That would go a long way to getting her back on track. But first… *Voilà!* A closet! With a pair of fluffy pink robes with rose-gold stitching and matching slippers, no less. *Viva Vallemont!*

She turned around. Will had moved to the lounge room and was sitting on the couch, looking right at home.

Sadie thought of the bath. Her head felt like mush. Her muscles ached. Even her bones were tired. Happy-go-lucky reserves fading like an empty battery, she said, "Give me ten minutes."

With that she headed into the bathroom.

There she stripped off Will's clothes and took off her chemise.

Something rubbed against her thigh. The garter. Thankfully the ring was still attached. Hugo's grandmother's ring. Not only was it part of the royal collection, and worth more than the building she was standing in, but also it didn't belong to her any more.

Not that it ever really had.

She carefully slid the garter down her leg and over her foot, placing it on the bathroom sink.

Last came her stockings, mud-covered and torn. Without a shred of remorse she threw them in the bin.

Then she turned the taps on the gorgeous big bath to as hot as was manageable. She found complimentary bubbles and squeezed until the bottle was empty and watched as the room became misty with steam and the bubbles threatened to topple over the sides.

And, as water tended to do, it began to unlock and unwind the knotty thoughts, opening the way to the simplest plan for dealing with the problem in front of her—moving Dr Will Darcy on.

Will leant back into the big, soft couch, checked his watch and adjusted the map of his day yet again.

He hadn't given up on making the late flight home, even as the afternoon faded, but then evening began to creep in, painting golden tracts of sunlight across the wooden floor.

It flipped a memory to the front of the pack. A crumbling cottage made of stone; cosy and warm, with a fireplace and rugs on the wooden floor. His parents' house—his and Clair's—before his mother and father had died.

His grandmother had insisted he'd dreamt it. No Darcy would dare live in such a place.

But something about this place made the memory feel solid. Perhaps it was the surrealism of events. Or the fact he was thinking so much about Clair.

He rubbed his hands over his face, then reached for his phone, dashing off a quick message to Hugo giving him their location.

Within seconds a message came back:

Well done.

As if he'd known Sadie-wrangling wouldn't be easy.

Needing a distraction, Hugo made another call.

The phone was answered. "Boss man!"

"Natalie. How are you?"

"Frantic. Busy. Overworked."

"Happy to hear it."

Will's assistant laughed, the jolly sound coming to him from somewhere in the Midwest of the United States.

Natalie had worked for him going on seven years now, after having been attached to his case by a publicity firm the week his textbook was first published. Finding her tough, keen and pedantic, he'd offered her a permanent position as his assistant and she'd snapped it up. They'd never actually met, working purely online and over the phone which suited him. Less time wasted on personal chit chat that way. She ran his bookings, planned his travel and was the gatekeeper between him and his business manager, clients, institutions, conglomerates and governments the world over.

"Now," said Natalie, "Garry is breathing down my neck like a dragon with a blocked nose, wanting to set up a meeting."

Will's business manager. Probably wanting to talk career strategy, aka Slow Down Before You Break Down. He'd heard it before, mostly from whoever he was dating at the time. Perhaps it was time for a new business manager too.

"When are you coming home?"

Will knew that by "home" Natalie didn't mean London. He had an apartment there, as he did in New Mexico, Sweden, Chile and many of the best star-gazing spots in the world, but he was rarely in one place longer than any other. By "When are you coming home?" Natalie meant, when was he getting back to work?

"What's coming up?"

Natalie listed a string of upcoming engagements. Full to bursting. Just as he liked it.

Without the onus of family, his work was the sun around which his life revolved. Whether he was looking through a telescope, hooking a crowd of eager-faced college students, putting the hard word on funding to a room filled with industry leaders, chipping away at the whys and wherefores of the universe, he was as engrossed now as he ever had been.

The rare times he loosened his grip, took a short break, said no to opportunity, he felt his life touching on the ordinary—and with it a creeping sense of futility. Of being indolent and inadequate. Just as his grandmother assured him his parents had been.

"You've also had meeting and speaking requests from a talk show in LA, a finishing school in the south of France, and…this is my favourite." She rattled off the name of a big-time rapper, who was keen on investing in new digital mirroring technology that Will had funded from day dot. NASA were liking the looks of it and the musician wanted in.

"Fit them in."

Not surprised with his answer, Natalie barrelled on. "And the prime minister would like five minutes next week."

Will perked up. "The agenda?"

He could all but see Natalie's grin as she said, "The Templeton Grant."

Will smacked his hand on his thigh. "Finally! Make the time. Day or night. I'm there."

Professor Templeton was the man who had conducted the first lecture Will had ever attended. He had become a mentor over the years until he had passed away a few months before. The long-running grant the professor had directed for the university was in danger of being phased out. Will was determined not to let that happen. He'd petitioned parliament to ask they continue in perpetuity, and to rename it in Templeton's honour. So far unsuccessfully. The prime minister—a smart man, a good man, a man of science—was his last hope.

"You bet," said Natalie. And Will was certain she'd make it work.

Until then, so long as he was on the first plane out in the morning, he could roll from one commitment to the next like the human tumbleweed that he was.

"Anything else I can do for you, Boss Man?" Natalie asked.

"Tell Garry we'll make time soon. And send

through the changes to the calendar when you have them."

"Shall do." A beat then. "So is it true?"

"What's that?"

"That the royal wedding didn't go off as planned?" Her sing-song voice dropped, as if they were sitting across from one another at a café. "It's all over the news. Apparently, the bride-to-be had a change of heart."

"You don't say."

Will glanced towards the wooden door when the sound of running water stopped. He listened a moment before he heard a splash. He imagined Sadie stepping a muddy foot into the bath. Then a long, pale calf, then...

Natalie sighed, bringing his vision to a halt. "She looked so nice too. Fun. Smiley. Someone you could be friends with. What did you think? I mean, before she did a runner? Did she seem as lovely as she looked in the magazines?"

Will knew better than to engage. He rubbed his temple instead.

"Aw, come on, Boss Man! My cousin Brianna works for a reality TV producer. I don't get many chances to one-up her in ways she understands."

"Alas."

"Fine. I'm guessing by the stoic silence she's not all she's cracked up to be. I mean, did you get a load of the Prince? Oh, me…oh, my. I guess a real-life, normal girl marrying a prince is simply too much to hope for."

"Hang in there, Natalie."

"I'm all right. You're the only man I need."

"Lucky me."

And then she was gone.

It seemed word was out. If Natalie was busy making negative assumptions, tucked away in her cottage in Wisconsin, it wasn't looking good. Things had gone up a notch. This was no longer simply a case of keeping Sadie in sight until Hugo came to get her, but actually keeping her safe.

Something he'd not been able to do for Clair.

Throat feeling unnaturally tight, Will lifted a hand to his neck, tugged his tie loose, then pulled it free and tossed it on top of his bag.

He wasn't built for this. All this…emotional disarray. It wore down a man's sharp edges. He liked his edges. On a day like today—with the whole world looking to others with a need to "share"—those edges were a requirement.

Ironic that he'd thought Clair's memory would

be the biggest battle he'd fight today, instead it was the reality of Sadie. Yet somehow it was all intertwined. Choices, decisions, reactions, repercussions.

The door to the bathroom opened. He pulled himself to standing. Turned. And whatever ethical dilemma he'd been mulling over disintegrated into so many dust motes as his eyes found Sadie.

Gone was his oversized tracksuit, the piles of messy curls, the tear-soaked make-up.

Her hair was wet, and long, and straight. Her cheeks were pink from the heat of the bathroom. Freckles stood out on the bridge of her straight nose. Without the black make-up her eyes were even bigger. *Blue*, he thought, catching glints of sky. Wrapped in a big, fluffy, shapeless robe, she seemed taller. Upright. More graceful somehow. Long, lean and empirically lovely.

Something tightened in his gut at the sight of her. Something raw and unsettling and new. Like the deep ache of a fresh bruise.

Her brow knotted and she ran a self-conscious hand over her hair.

Will came to; realised he'd been staring.

"Better?" he asked.

"Much. I did wonder if you'd still be here when I got out."

Will held out his hands. "Not going anywhere without my favourite running gear."

Sadie seemed to remember she was holding his clothes. She padded over towards him and handed them over. She was careful not to touch him.

He threw them atop his bag and her eyes followed, glaring at the clothes as if by sheer force of will alone she could unzip his bag, pack the clothes away and make him leave.

"Now that you have them..."

Will put his hands into his pockets. Right. How to convince her to let him stay without coming across as a Neanderthal. Or a Lothario. Without giving her actual cause to run.

"Will," she said.

"Yes, Sadie."

She lifted her gaze, bright eyes snagging on his. Then she laughed, a sound both sweet and husky. But there was no humour in it. "I was going to eke it out. To keep you hanging. Make you suffer. But you look like you're about to pull a muscle with the effort at keeping this up. I saw your credit card downstairs. You're Will Darcy.

You were heading to the wedding at the palace today because you were invited by Prince Alessandro himself."

Will should have been prepared for this eventuality. He was a man of angles after all. And control was an illusion. The universe chaotic. Any number of factors altered the possible futures of any given body, making accurate projections near impossible. Still, he found himself unprepared.

"Are you going to deny it?" she asked; gaze steady, that humming energy of hers now turned up to eleven.

He shook his head, *No.*

As if she'd been hoping for a different answer, Sadie deflated, crumpling to sit on the arm of the couch. "Okay. Next question. I know the answer but I want to hear it from you. Do you know who I am?"

Will crossed his arms over his chest as he decided how to play this; fast and loose as he had so far, or absolute truth. As a man of science, the decision was elementary, and a relief.

"You were Hugo's intended. Now you are his runaway bride."

Her eyes were wide, luminous in the fading light. "How?"

"The dress. The tears. The determination to be as far from the palace as you could be. But it was the ring that clinched it. I'd seen it before. We were at school when his grandmother sent it to him. After..."

"After Prince Karl—Hugo's father—died in a crash," she finished, her gaze not shifting a jot. She was far tougher than she looked.

Then she shifted, her robe falling open. The slit separated at her ankles, then her knees, revealing one long, creamy pale leg. She had freckles on her knees. A small bruise just below. Her hands delved up inside the robe and, before Will could even look away, with a wriggle she pulled a frilly pink garter down her leg.

The fact that this rather intimate move had been meant for Hugo later that evening was not lost on him. Neither was the heat that travelled through him like a rogue wave.

Will pressed his feet harder into the floor and thought of England.

Holding the garter scrunched in her hand, she took a deep breath and opened her palm. And there, tied to the thing with a length of pink ribbon, was the Ring of Vallemont.

Then, tucking the ring back into her palm, she

held out her other hand. "Mercedes Gray Leonine. Pleased to meet you."

He took it. Her hand wrapped around his—soft and cool and impossibly fine. He could all but feel the blood pulsing beneath her skin, the steady vibration of the perpetual electric impulses that made her tick.

His voice was a little rough as he said, "Will Darcy. Pleasure's all mine."

She let go and used both hands to slide the garter back into place. "But it's not your pleasure, not really, is it?"

Will said nothing, holding his breath so long it grew stale in his lungs.

"I'm a drama teacher, you know. Or I was…before. Body language—understanding it and duplicating it—is my job. You've hardly hidden the fact that you would rather be anywhere but here." She blinked at him. "If it helps any, I'd rather be pretty much anywhere but here too."

It didn't. It only made his task more complicated than it already was. He didn't want to see her side of things. He certainly didn't want to empathise. He wanted to keep her from running away again and gift her back to Hugo in one piece. Then leave.

He saw the moment she realised it too. She sat taller, and narrowed her eyes his way. Something hardened in her gaze, like steel tempered by fire. And Will couldn't press his feet into the floor hard enough.

Her eyes drilled into his as she said, "He'd never mentioned you before, you know."

A deliberate barb, it scored a direct hit. Will crossed his arms tighter.

She noticed. A small smile tugged at one corner of her mouth. "And suddenly, with the wedding, you loomed large. This friend from school he hadn't seen in years. A falling-out he never explained, no matter how maddeningly I prodded. With all that, I imagined you hunched and brooding. More Holden Caulfield, less…"

"Less?"

"Mr Rochester." She waved a hand his way as if it was obvious, her eyes dashing from his chest to his hair and back to his face. Her cheeks came over such a sudden pink he knew he'd have to track down this Rochester fellow the moment he had the chance.

She looked down at her toes, where he could see the nails painted in some kind of animal print, making him wonder if this palace rebellion of hers had been coming on for some time. Then she asked, "How did you imagine me?"

"I didn't." It was true. He'd done everything in his power not to know anything about her. He was no masochist. Though the longer he chose to stick around this woman, the more he'd question that fact.

Sadie crossed her arms, mirroring his defensive position. "Seriously? Then you have a better hold over your curiosity than I do. Well, how about now? Am I the kind of girl you imagined Hugo would one day marry?"

Will ran a hand through his hair. Hell. This was worse than masochism. He'd found himself on the pathway to hell.

"Forget it. It doesn't matter," she said, shaking her head. "Okay. So, cards-on-the-table time. What are we doing here, Will? What's your end game? I know something happened between you and Hugo, something regrettable. If your intentions aren't above reproach, if you're out to humiliate him in any way... I'll... I'll cut off your whatsit."

Even though he knew she was all bluff, Will's whatsit twitched in response. "I think he's had quite enough humiliating for one day, don't you?"

Her gaze dropped to his…whatsit.

Will's voice was dry as he said, "I was talking about Hugo."

Another hit. This one flashed in her eyes like a bonfire. "Leave him out of this."

He shook his head.

"Why? Wait. Have you spoken to him? Is he okay? Does he know we're here?"

Will pulled the phone from his pocket. "Call him. Ask him yourself."

Sadie's arms loosened, her hands dropping to grip the arms of the couch on which she sat. She pulled herself to standing. Then reached out and took Will's phone.

Their fingers brushed, static electricity crackling through his hand.

Her eyes shot to his. She'd felt it too. Breathing out hard, she asked, "Are you sure? I mean, will he even take my call?"

"Call him."

She nodded and took a few steps away, before turning back.

"Today—not going through with the wedding… It wasn't a decision I made lightly. I usually make a much better first impression. I'm very likeable, you know."

"I'm sure."

She looked at him then, all ocean-blue eyes and electric energy. With her brow twitching a moment, she said, "No, you're not."

And then she stepped out onto the balcony and was once more gone from his sight.

With leaden feet, Will sat back on the couch. Feeling like he'd gone ten rounds.

She was right. After what she'd done today, to his oldest friend, he wasn't convinced that he would ever come to like her. But there was no denying she'd made an impression he'd not soon forget.

CHAPTER FIVE

SADIE'S HEART STAMMERED against her ribs.

In front of her, the palace was glowing gold in the final throes of the dying light.

Through the gauzy curtains behind her, a man was all but keeping her hostage. A man who'd made no bones about the fact he wasn't a fan. A man who made her feel unsettled and antsy and contrite.

And in her hands was a link to her Prince. Her friend. The man she'd wronged.

With the fall of night came a brisk wintry breeze cascading off the snow-topped mountains in the distance, skipping and swirling through the narrow valley and tossing Sadie's damp hair about her shoulders.

She pulled her gown tighter, sat on a small wrought-iron chair and tucked her feet up beneath her. And typed in Hugo's private number.

As unexpected as it was sudden, Hugo's picture flashed onto Will's screen as the phone rang. Will was in it too. They had their arms around one another as they stood atop a mountain somewhere. Young men. Grinning. Happier times.

The phone stopped ringing.

"Darcy?" said Hugo, in his deep bass voice. "What's happened?"

Sadie pictured him sitting behind the grand old desk in his study, foot hooked up on the other knee, hand gripping his chin.

Sadie closed her eyes and swallowed. "Hugo—" Her voice cracked. She cleared her throat. "Hugo, it's me."

Sadie couldn't remember a time when she'd been so scared of a response. Not since calling her mother to let her know New York hadn't worked out as hoped and that she was coming home.

She'd felt like a failure then. As though she'd let everyone down. Right now, she *knew* she was a failure. She *knew* she'd let everyone down.

Finally he spoke. "Leo."

Sadie nearly sobbed with relief. Hugo was the only person in the entire world who called her that and the fact he used her nickname now meant so much. It meant everything.

"Hey, big guy. How's it hanging?"

"Tight and away."

Her laughter was croaky. "Yeah. Figured as much. I'm assuming you got my note?"

"The one about deciding not to marry me after all?"

"That's the one."

The moment she'd realised there was no way she could go through with the wedding, she'd also known she couldn't go without letting him know.

Finding him would have been impossible without making a huge scene. At the time not embarrassing Hugo in public had seemed the most important thing. Now she realised she'd simply postponed the inevitable.

So she'd torn a page from a hymnal, grabbed a stick of lipstick left behind by the make-up artist and scribbled down the best short explanation she could. She'd given it to the sweet maid who'd been left to "keep her company" and, using every ounce of charisma she had in her arsenal, had convinced the young girl to deliver it to the Prince.

Then she'd climbed out of the old stone window and run.

"The poor girl who gave it to me was so terrified she left fingerprints in the thing."

Sadie laughed, even as a rogue tear slithered down her cheek. She dashed it away with the sleeve of her gown. "She needs a raise. A big one." Then, "Is it crazy over there?"

"That's one way of putting it. It was agreed that Aunt Marguerite would make the announcement to the guests. One line—the wedding would not go ahead but the after-party would. Then everyone was promptly herded into the ballroom. The champagne is flowing. The music is loud. The doors are bolted shut."

"She's hoping they'll not remember any of it in the morning?"

"Very much."

Sadie heard a squeak. He was definitely in the leather chair behind his desk. She wished she was in there now, lying on the big, soft rug, using a throw cushion as a headrest, annoying him as he tried to work; chatting about her latest class play or Netflix addiction; niggling him about some movie star who'd claimed to have a crush on him; listening as he took calls from foreign leaders, or those interested in his divine resorts.

"So," he said, his voice nothing but a rumble. "You've met Darcy."

"Mmm-hmm." Suddenly uncomfortable, Sadie

adjusted her gown. Then her sitting posture. Then the garter which had begun to feel scratchy now her tights were gone.

"What do you think?"

"About?"

Hugo waited. No surprise that he saw right through her. Born two years apart to the day, they'd grown up in one another's pockets. The Prince and the daughter of a palace maid. As the story went, she'd told anyone who would listen that she'd one day marry Hugo before she could even pronounce his real name properly.

"Oh," said Sadie, "you mean Will? He's..." *dogged, grouchy, brooding, infuriating, enigmatic* "...a very good driver."

Hugo's chuckle was pained. "You playing nice?"

"Of course I am! I'm the epitome of nice. Ask anyone." A beat. "Well, maybe give it a few days." *Weeks. Months. Millennia.* "I'm not sure there's a person in the world who'd have a good thing to say about me right now. Hugo—"

"Leo. It's okay."

"But—"

"Truly."

"No. I need to say it. I wronged you. Terribly. I screwed up more than even I ever imagined I could and that's saying something. And I plan to do everything in my power to fix it. I'll write an official apology to the palace. I'll take out a full-page ad in the *Vallemont Chronicle*. I'll go door to door telling every man, woman and child that my running away had nothing to do with you. That you are the Prince they know you to be, while I am a complete flake. Anything."

"Anything except marry me."

She opened her mouth to…what? Tell him to give her another chance? That this time she could go through with it, if it was what he really wanted. What he needed. But for some reason Will's face popped into her head right at that moment. Those intensely dark eyes of his boring into her as if he'd accept nothing but the truth. Her truth. However unpopular it might be.

The tears flowed fast and furious now. "God, no. Anything except that."

Hugo laughed, as she'd known he would. Never in the history of history had there been a better man, meaning that he deserved a better woman.

Sadie shifted on the seat. "He doesn't like me, you know."

"Who?"

Right. They hadn't been talking about him,

she'd just been thinking about him. "Your old friend, Will Darcy."

"Not possible."

"Something to do with my actions today, perhaps?" But even as she said it, Sadie knew it wasn't that. Not entirely. It was something deeper. Something about her made him uneasy. Not what she'd done but who she was. And to think she'd thought she couldn't feel worse!

"I know you. Making people feel comfortable is your special skill. You'll work him until he adores you. You always do."

"Alas, once I give him his phone back he's outta here." No response from Hugo. Which gave her pause. "Unless I'm missing something."

"I'd like him to stay."

Sadie sat up so fast she nearly fell off the chair. The thought of being *stuck* in the hotel room with Will—"working him until he adored her", no less—made her feel itchy all over.

"Hugo—"

"I'd feel better knowing that you had company. At least until I can send for you."

"A babysitter, you mean. So that I don't get up to more mischief than I already have."

"If you like."

The ease of his about-turn gave him away. "You don't think I need a babysitter. You think I need a bodyguard."

How bad was it out there? For the first time since she'd run she wanted access to a TV. She remembered Janine from downstairs saying "the honeymoon suite" didn't have one. Maybe she could ask Will if she could check out the news pages on his phone.

"Send Prospero," she tried, imagining Hugo's big, neckless, mountain-sized, actual bodyguard.

"Prospero wouldn't leave me if ordered him to by royal decree. It has to be Will."

She dropped her forehead into her hand.

"Humour me," Hugo said.

He didn't say, *You owe me this much at least*, but Sadie read between the lines. He'd been born into a royal bloodline, a flourishing principality run by very smart, savvy, forward-thinking people. Hugo could be a master manipulator when he wanted to.

If making things right meant having to put up with Will Darcy's disquieting presence, then Sadie would just have to handle it.

"And what would you like me to tell your friend

about this arrangement? Not my biggest fan, re-member."

"Just tell him I asked."

"Really? He doesn't come across as the kind of man who blindly follows."

"Just tell him."

"Fine. And when things die down? What then?"

"Then I'll send someone to bring you home."

Home.

Sadie stifled a whimper.

That Hugo could sit there, in the middle of the scandal of his life, and truly believe she could ever move back into his venerable ancestral home after what she'd done… He was the best man she'd ever known times ten.

"Anything you need until then?" he asked.

Clothes. A phone. Money. Her mum. A hug. A new place to live. For her students not to be out there thinking badly of her. For the people who knew her best to believe she'd had no choice. For the world to forget her name.

"I'm fine."

"As for Will?"

"Mmm?"

"Take it easy on the guy. If he's the same man I

knew back then, he comes across as a big, gruff loner, but deep down he's a good guy."

"It'd have to be *waaaay* deep down."

"Leo."

"Fine! I'll be sweetness and light."

"I know you will. Now… Sorry. Hang on a moment." Hugo put her on hold.

The village below was quiet in the looming gloom of late autumnal dusk. Through the curled iron of the balcony she watched a small, battered Fiat bump slowly along the street below. When a group of revellers pushed their way out the front door of a pub down the road, she ducked down so they wouldn't see her.

And she suddenly felt terribly alone.

But while he had people clamouring to do his bidding, Hugo was far more alone than she was. He always had been. It came with the position, with the expectations thrust upon him from birth, with not knowing if people liked you for who you were or what you had to offer. And now, without her at his side, she feared he always would be.

Was that why she'd planned to marry him? Maybe. Partly. If so, at one time it had seemed like reason enough.

After a most inauspicious entry into the world, Sadie's life had been blessed.

Educated by royal tutors. Given music lessons, dance lessons, drama lessons. During the latter, she'd discovered the direct link between putting on a show and having people look to her with smiles on their faces. Thus her love of theatre had been born.

But who deserved that kind of luck? Truly? People who earned it, who were grateful for every ounce; who were nice and kind and likeable; who made sure not to let down all those who'd been instrumental in giving her the chances she'd had.

The Muzak stopped as Hugo came back on the line. "Apologies. It was Aunt Marguerite."

"Ruing the day she rescued my mother and me?"

"Asking if you are all right."

Of course. "What did you tell her?"

"That if you're not yet, you soon will be."

Sadie let her feet drop to the ground, the freezing cold tiles keeping her in the here and now.

"I should go," Hugo said.

"Me too. Busy, busy! You don't have to send someone for me, you know. I'm a big girl."

"I don't have to, but I want to."

Her eyes fell closed. Giving him that was the least she could do. "Do it soon."

"As soon as I'm able. Stay safe."

With that, Hugo rang off.

Sadie uncurled herself from the chair, shivering as she stood. The temperature had dropped fast as night closed in quickly. The sky was now a soft dusty blue, the mountains guarding the borders of her tiny country glowing white.

Just before she turned to head back inside, the first star popped into sight. She thought about making a wish, but had no idea what to wish for.

Will was on the couch, one foot hooked over the other knee, fingers running back and forth over his chin.

He looked up at the sound of the French door sliding closed, a slice of moonlight cutting his strong face in half. "All's well in the state of Denmark?"

Sadie's mouth twitched. She could count on one finger the number of men who'd quoted Shakespeare at her without knowing what a geek-fan she was.

She walked over to Will and gave him back his phone, then took a seat on the other couch. "Princess Marguerite is hosting the party to end all parties in the hope of either giving everyone the night of their lives so they leave with only good to say, or they are too hungover to speak of it."

"Seems a pity to be missing it."

Sadie coughed out a bitter laugh. "For some strange reason, I'm struggling to imagine you partying. You seem a little straight for all that. More of a cognac and non-fiction tome kind of guy."

Will breathed out hard, his hands coming together, fingers running over fingers in a hypnotic pattern. "Is that what you came in here to say?"

Well, no. But it had felt good to have a dig at the guy anyway. Hugo clearly thought more highly of her "working it" skills than she did.

Enough dilly-dallying. Time to get this over with. Hugo seemed to think Will would stay simply because he'd asked him to. Hugo believed Will was a good guy. And that had to count for something.

So, while the words felt like stones in her mouth, she managed to say, "While I feel like I'm taking the feminist movement back decades by asking this, is there any chance you could stick around until Hugo sends someone to whisk me out of here?"

Will sat forward. His hand went to his watch—big, fancy, classy—twisting it about his wrist as he made his decision.

It hadn't occurred to her until that moment that he might say no—claim work, or play; claim a jealous wife or a sick child or a job that needed him more. That he might leave her here, in this honeymoon suite with its princess bed and its view of the palace.

"And how long might that be?"

"I…don't know. As soon as humanly possible."

"Is this a request from you, or Hugo?"

"Does it matter?"

The slight tilt of his head told her it did.

Well, buddy, you rub me up the wrong way too. The funny thing was, though, sitting there beside him, her hairs standing on end, a tornado in her tummy, prickling under the burn of his hot, hard gaze, being on his bad side felt like the safer option.

Sadie shuffled forward on the chair, held her hands out in supplication and said, "Look, I get that I'm not your favourite person."

There, now it was out there. Maybe that would alleviate the tension sapping the air from the room.

"But neither am I some damsel in distress, if that's what you think."

To that he said nothing.

"The truth is, you don't know me. You just happened upon me at just about the crappiest moment of my entire life. And now I'm exhausted. And hungry. And stuck in a hotel room with a stranger. Which isn't going to bring out my best. I promised Hugo I'd be sweetness and light, but I'm not sure how long I can keep that up. So, stay, don't stay; right now I'm done caring."

Will looked cool as a cucumber as he said, "Is self-sabotage a habit of yours?"

"*Excuse* me?"

"I'm simply going by the evidence. I've known you a couple of hours and in that time you've rejected a prince and done your all to convince me to throw my hands in the air and give up on you."

"I'm not! I—"

"Then my staying won't bother you."

Oh.

"Not a jot," she said.

She lied. *He* bothered her. But that was just the price she had to pay.

"Then that's that," said Will.

Sadie breathed out hard and flopped back into

the couch, feeling better about having a plan, even if it wasn't hers.

Will opened up his battered silver bag to pull out a laptop. He flipped it open, long fingers tapping in a password. "Now, if you don't mind, I'm going to get some work done."

Sadie flapped a hand his way, barely wasting a thought wondering what that work might be. He was a doctor of some sort. Did they give doctorates in such pedantic things as forensic accounting, or comment moderating?

She closed her eyes for a second. When she peeled her eyes open—five seconds later, or five minutes, she couldn't be sure—it was to find Will looking at her strangely.

Sadie followed the path of his gaze to find her gown had fallen open. Not much—enough to show her collarbone and a little shoulder. Maybe a swell of something more, but nothing to get excited about.

When she found his eyes again his jaw clenched, as hard as stone. His nostrils flared with the fervour of a racehorse, then with patent effort tore his gaze away.

Sadie was surprised to find her hands shaking as she surreptitiously tugged her dressing gown back together. And her heart beat like gang-busters.

He didn't like her. But it turned out he was very much aware of her.

The horrible truth was that she was aware of him too. The sure strength of his arms, the scent of his neck, the intensity of his gaze had been playing like a brutal loop in the back of her mind whenever she felt herself begin to relax.

And now they were stuck here, in this romantic hotel room.

It was going to be a long night.

Sadie had fallen asleep on the couch almost instantly.

A few hours later she lay there still, breathing softly through open lips, her lashes creating dark smudges beneath her eyes. Her gown...

Will looked away from her dressing gown and ran a hand over his face. A move he'd made so much in the past day he was in danger of rearranging his features permanently.

Will refocused on his laptop—not that it looked any different from the way it had ten minutes before. The internet was prohibitively slow, meaning he couldn't check Natalie's updates to his calendar. Or access Hubble's latest infrared take on Orion that was due to land, eyes only, that morning. Or open the latest incarnation of the Orion's Sword game sitting temptingly in his inbox.

And he'd had no word from Hugo.

Edgy and frustrated, Will rolled his shoulders, got up, started a fire and checked out the kitchen, to find only a few mini-bar items. He could have done with some real food, but, since he wasn't lucky enough to be at the non-wedding reception—aka the party to end all parties—he had to make do with instant coffee and a bar of chocolate-covered ginger.

The fire made short work of the cold room, so, needing some fresh air, Will headed to the balcony. The village was spread beneath him like something on the front of a Marks and Spencer biscuit tin.

Sipping on the bitter brew, he looked up. And promptly forgot to swallow.

For the perfect day had given way to an even more perfect night.

The combination of minimal light pollution from the old-fashioned gas lamps below, the elevated position of the hillside hotel and a first-quarter moon had made the galaxy come out to play.

From his cramped position tucked into the corner of the small balcony, Will found a nice angle on his target and racked up the focus.

His serious telescope—with long exposure CCD camera attachment—which lived in the permanent glass box atop his London town house, had collected more detailed images of the nebula's famous irregular, translucent fan-shaped cloud, and ultraviolet glow. But this telescope—smaller, older, less sophisticated—was the one he took with him all over the world.

It was the last gift he'd received from Clair.

He'd added to it over the years. Modified it to keep it relevant. And right now, as always, it did right by him, giving him a really nice shot of vivid grey-green mist enshrouding a distant star.

But what he was really hoping for was—any moment now— *There!* A shooting star. And another. The annual Orionid Meteor Shower in all its glory.

Will sat back in the freezing wrought-iron chair

and did something he rarely took the time to do nowadays: he watched the sky with his own two eyes. The moment seemed to require it.

It was late. A ways after midnight. And the entire world felt quiet. Still. Slumberous and safe within the cradle of jagged mountains all around. It was as though this spot had a direct link to the heavens.

"Will?" Sadie's voice cut through his thoughts.

His chair scraped sharply against the tiled floor of the small balcony as Will arose.

Sadie stood in the French windows, nibbling on a bag of peanuts. "What are you doing out here? It's freezing. You should… Oh." Her eyes widened comically as she spotted the apparatus taking up most of the balcony. She stepped out onto the tiles, wincing at the cold beneath her bare feet. "Was this here the whole time?"

Will laughed, the rough sound drifting away into the darkness. "I brought her with me."

"Her?"

Will put a hand on the body of the telescope. "Sadie, this is Maia. Maia—Sadie."

"Pretty name. An old flame?"

"A young star. Found on the shoulder of Taurus." Will pointed unerringly towards the bull constellation without even having to look.

"So *that's* what you had hiding in your silver case! By the measly contents of your other bag I'd have bet you were planning on skedaddling tomorrow at the very latest. And yet you lugged this thing all the way here? Why?"

"Did Hugo not mention what I do for a living?"

She grimaced. "No. Maybe. He mostly told stories about your time at school. How you led him to the dark side, teaching him how best to ditch class. Or the time he dared you to petition the school to reinstate Domestic Science and you won. So many *Boys' Own* adventure stories I may have drifted off now and then." Her eyes darted to the telescope and back again. "So…this. This is what you do? What are you? Some kind of… *astronomer*?"

Will nodded.

And Sadie's eyes near bugged out of her head. "Really? But that's so cool! I imagined you in a career that was more…phlegmatic. No offence."

None taken. In fact, he took it as a compliment. A high level of impassivity was necessary to doing his best work. Besides, Will was too busy noticing she seemed to imagine him a fair bit. But he kept that noticing to himself.

"Hugo's friends are all in their family business—money, politics, ruling." She scrunched up her nose. "But not you. Unless astronomy *is* your family business...?"

"My family business was holding on tight to old money. And my grandmother's version of ruling was browbeating the butlers until they quit. This seemed a better choice."

Her hair rippled in the light breeze. "I would have thought that kind of thing was done by computers nowadays. Super-robots."

"Computers can certainly extrapolate data, make comparisons, find patterns in big, random, violent actualities that rise and fall over billions of years before we've even seen their first spark of light in our sky. But—as my old university mentor, Professor Templeton, used to remind us—the first step, the human element in all that, is to wonder."

"I like the sound of your professor."

"He was one of the good ones."

"You've surprised me just now, Will Darcy. Quite a bit. So what are you looking for?"

"That's a big question."

Sadie laughed. And waggled her fingers at the telescope.

"Ah," said Will. "You mean in there."

She laughed again, her eyes gleaming. The quiet, the dark, the late hour…they all promoted a sense of playfulness. Or maybe that was simply her: mischievous, bright, irreverent, with an agile open mind.

Will rubbed a hand over his chin to find it rough. Somehow he'd forgotten his nightly shave. Reminding himself to fix that tomorrow, he said, "This telescope isn't big enough for any serious research. I bring it with me more out of sentimentality than anything else."

"You? Sentimental?"

"Apparently so. It was a gift." *Swallow.* "From my sister." He braced himself against the jagged knot tightening in his belly. Then he moved on. "What would you like to see?"

"Me? Wow. I suddenly feel really ignorant. I don't know all that much about what's out there apart from, you know, moon, stars. The earth is the centre of the universe."

Will's mouth twitched. Then he leaned down, adjusted direction and focus and found the general direction of his telescope's namesake. Then he pushed back the chair, and motioned for Sadie to have a look.

Adjusting her robe, Sadie shuffled in closer to the telescope. Will had to press himself hard against the railing so as not to be right behind her as, fingers lightly gripping the eyepiece, she bent to have a look.

Sadie's mouth stretched into a slow smile. "Oh. Oh, Will. That is…spectacular."

"Pleiades," he said. "Otherwise known as the Seven Sisters. Maia is the fourth brightest."

She stood and blinked up into the cosmos. "Show me more. Show me your very favourite thing out there. Show me something that makes a man like you gasp with delight."

Will cocked an eyebrow. "I'm not sure I've ever gasped, in delight or otherwise."

Her grin was bright, even in the low moonlight. "Maybe you're just not doing it right." She flicked a glance to the sky. "Maybe you could lighten up a little. Put that frown of yours away for a bit and find the delight. Maybe you just have to look harder."

He looked, but not at the sky. At her profile, open and bright. At the dishevelled way she'd tied her gown. At her leopard-print toenails as her toes curled into the cold floor.

For the first time since Natalie had rung him about the invitation, Will purposely wondered about the girl Hugo had planned to marry, opening the part of himself he preferred to keep under lock and key—that place that bred *what ifs* and *if onlys*.

It was his turn to imagine as he attempted to picture the Hugo he knew with this restive, indefatigable, unkempt creature.

And couldn't.

Deep down in a place both unfamiliar and disquieting, Will wondered how Hugo could have chosen a woman who was so clearly not meant for him.

Will cleared his throat and did a mental about-turn.

Nothing was *meant* in this world. Nothing was for ever. Planets collided, suns faded, worlds were destroyed by their own cores, imploding in on themselves in utter self-destruction. The universe was random and chaotic and it was foolish to think otherwise.

"Move aside." He gave her a nudge with his hip so that he might shift the telescope a smidgeon.

"Should I prepare myself to be amazed?" she asked as they swapped places again, this time the front of her dressing gown brushing against his arm. His hairs stood on end, chasing the sensation.

His voice was gruff as he said, "I would think the purpose of preparation was to avoid surprise."

"We shall see," she said. This time Sadie held her breath. Her voice revenant, she whispered, "What am I looking at now?"

"That would be Orion. A diffuse nebula in the Milky Way. Around one thousand five hundred light-years from here and containing thousands of stars, it is the nearest star-forming region to Earth."

Will had heard Orion, so optically beautiful, described as "angel's breath against a frosted sky". He believed its true beauty was that it was their best glimpse into how the universe had begun.

Sadie pulled back. She looked up at the sky for a good while. Then, her voice rusty, she said, "I can't even find the words, Will. It's beautiful, to be sure. But also…somehow hollow. Like if you look at it too long, all that darkness would see your darkness until it becomes one. 'Stars, hide your fires; Let not light see my black and deep desires.'"

Her last words had been so soft he wasn't even sure she'd meant to say them out loud. The order tickled at the corner of Will's brain. He sorted through the databanks of information he'd stored over the years and found a match. *Macbeth.*

Catalogued under cosmic quotes he'd kept note of over the years, he found, "'When beggars die there are no comets seen; The heavens themselves blaze forth the death of princes.'"

She blinked as if coming out of a trance, then turned to him, incredulous. "Seriously?"

"Seriously what?"

"You're quoting Shakespeare. Again."

"I'm very well-read."

"I'm beginning to see that." She shook her head. "Because that's my thing, you know. My mission in life is to show attention-deficient young adults how to concentrate long enough to get through an entire Shakespearean play. Huh. I just realised. Will. Will Shakespeare. You have the same name."

As her gaze held his and didn't let go, Will felt the air shift between them. A wind of change. A disturbance in the force. Electric currents zapped and collided until he was all but sure he'd see sparks.

But deeper, beneath it all, a sense of recognition; of shared experience; of lives lived parallel; of truth. Will felt its pull like a physical thing.

People spoke of chemistry being the reason people were drawn to one another. But it was gravity that caused one body to revolve around another. That said the denser gravity of a planet could draw on the lesser gravity of a meteor, leading to destruction, sometimes on a grand scale.

Sadie's gaze snapped to something over his shoulder.

"Did you see that?" Sadie gasped. "Keep watching. Keep watching... There!"

Will looked up. He watched as another shooting star flashed, flew and disappeared, disintegrating into a mass of scattered space dust.

If he'd believed in such things he might have taken it as a sign.

CHAPTER SIX

SADIE WOKE UP with a start.

It was deep in the heart of the witching hour; that time of night when every sound, every thought felt heightened. Her skin prickled with sweat. Unfamiliar sheets twisted around her legs. Her chemise had ridden high enough to nearly strangle her.

She wriggled and rolled, kicking off blankets, and scrambled up towards a mound of pillows. Holding her legs to her chest, she stared into the semi-darkness. Embers crackled in the fireplace below, the eerie golden glow casting light and shadow over the room. And over the man sleeping on the couch.

She couldn't make out much detail bar one bare arm dangling off the edge, fingertips nearly grazing the floor. A large naked foot hooked over the arm rest.

It was more than enough.

She looked away, towards the French door, towards the palace; towards her bed, her pillow, her home. She wondered if Hugo had managed to fall asleep or if he was still awake, lamenting what might have been, or relieved she'd let him off the hook.

She slid back down into the big, soft bed, pulling her sheets up to her neck and trying to recapture her dream. But all she remembered were insubstantial threads, like ribbons in a storm.

A few moments later she lifted her head, checking to make sure Will was actually asleep. His arm lifted and fell, as if in time with long, slow breaths.

Whatever. Sleep or no sleep, as soon as Hugo sent someone to get her, chances were she'd never see Will again.

There hadn't exactly been time or opportunity to uncover why Will and Hugo had been estranged since school, despite the fact there was clearly great mutual respect. But it must have been significant. A great fight? A deep betrayal? Or had she simply read *Macbeth* so many times she saw potential drama everywhere she looked?

No. Something must have happened. In her experience, men didn't lash out like wounded animals unless they felt cornered.

Her father had been the first. Taking umbrage to the fact Sadie's mother had dared love his child as much as she loved him. For that he had left and not looked back.

Then there had been her acting coach in New York. An older man, a faded Paul Newman wannabe, he'd been her teacher, then her mentor, dangling the string of success for a couple of years. Once she'd bitten he'd become her agent. Not a good one, but the fact he'd seen something in her had felt like enough. Until the day he offered her a part—not the lead—in the "adult" film he was producing. When she'd refused, point blank, he'd kicked her to the kerb, leaving her homeless, the entire experience telling her it was time to head home.

She'd even seen how implacable Hugo could be, if those in his care were under attack. It was the very reason he'd wanted to marry her, after all.

Will's "self-sabotage" accusation hovered on the edge of her subconscious, but she brushed it away.

She'd heard them called "the rational sex", but in her experience men made decisions based on emotion over common sense far more than women.

From what she'd seen of Will Darcy so far, he'd not proven to be any different.

More awake than asleep now, Sadie laid herself out as flat as she could, becoming one with the mattress, and closed her eyes. She breathed slowly through her nose and wondered... Did Will dream? If so, of what? Supernovas and little green men? Or was he a classicist—dreaming of memory, hope, wishes, flying, falling, desire...

Just like that, her own dream came back to her in a rush. Hurtling through a sky filled with planets, a great, hot sun and bright, thrusting comets. Only she wasn't falling, she was being held. Protected. By a pair of strong, warm arms. While also being shown the moon and stars.

She grabbed a spare pillow and shoved it over her head.

Will woke feeling as if he'd been hit by a truck.

Every muscle, joint and bone ached from trying to curl six feet two inches onto an over-soft two-seater.

He pressed himself to sitting, then rubbed both hands hard over his face in an effort to put all the bits back into the right place.

Will checked his phone. It was a little after

seven. He had had eleven missed messages over-night. Not unusual. The stars were always out somewhere in the world. He listened to them all, took mental notes and sent word to Natalie how to deal with each.

She hadn't yet sent word about a meeting time with the prime minister regarding the Templeton Grant. He nudged her to make it the number-one priority.

The moment he'd heard the grant was in jeopardy he'd felt a strange compulsion, a knowledge deep in his bones, that he had to use the power of his reputation for more than simply work.

For Professor Templeton's gentle patience had been Will's deliverance at a time when things had gone either way, and it seemed only right that he make sure the next generation of students would have the chance to find their path as he did that long-ago day.

Following that one random astronomy class, Will had doubled up on his degree, joined as many research projects as would have him. He'd worked nights, checking the university's tele-scope minute by minute for whichever project needed data at the time. And eventually he'd earned the Templeton Grant himself for his independent study on the Orion Nebula. It had paid his way through university, in one fell swoop giving him complete independence from his grandparents and showing them he was neither indolent nor inadequate. He was bloody hardworking and exceedingly bright. Despite them.

Clair would have been the same, if she'd been given the chance. So what choice did Will have but to take every opportunity she'd never had?

Keeping watch over Sadie had nudged him off course, which was not a comfortable place for him to be. Nevertheless, after a prolonged beat, he sent another message to Natalie asking her to cancel or postpone—with apologies—everything he had on for the next twenty-four hours. To keep the day after that on standby. And please not to injure herself when she fell over in shock.

Then he threw his phone into his leather bag and stood.

He rolled his shoulders. Cricked his neck.

Glancing towards the raised platform, he could make out the lump of Sadie's form. Fast sleep.

Weak, dreary sunlight attempted to breach the curtains before seeming to give up.

Hunger gnawed at his belly. If Hugo wasn't

here soon he'd have to head out and source some real food.

But first…needs must.

He grabbed his leather bag and headed to the bathroom. Since he couldn't get there without passing Sadie's bed, he found her splayed on her stomach like a human starfish, one hand hanging off one side, a toe hanging off the other. The sheets were twisted around her and tugged from their moorings. Her hair was splayed out across the white sheets like a red wine spill.

An empty chocolate packet lay open on the bedside table. And below it, in a pile on the floor, was her dressing gown. Meaning beneath the twisted sheets she wore…

Will kept his eyes straight ahead as he moved into the bathroom and shut the door. Two minutes later he was stripped and standing beneath a hot shower. And he did what he always did near water: he closed his eyes and let his mind go.

It wasn't an unusual phenomenon that his most complete theories had come to him while in the shower. Having nothing else to worry about, the mind travelled in disparate directions and made random connections it would otherwise miss.

He waited for his mind to mull over tricky calculations he'd been asked to weigh in on. Or the three-dimensional graphics of the Orion Nebula the gaming team in Oxford were working on.

But instead his head filled with silken, wine-red hair, soft, cool skin, eyes so deep they seemed to go on for ever.

Jaw clenching, he dragged his tired eyes open.

So, no stream of consciousness, then. Purposeful analysis was the order of the day. He began, as he always did, with known data.

Fact: he'd been on edge for days. Weeks even. Knowing he was set to face Hugo, to face his part in the derailment of their friendship, knowing that watching someone else take his sister's place at Hugo's side would be...difficult. No, it would be insufferable.

Fact: stress led to surges of adrenaline, a natural human response to an extraordinary amount of stimuli. Biological readiness for a fight or flight led to heightened senses. Which then led to a natural physical response to the attractive woman he was sharing a hotel room with.

Fact: he clearly wasn't the only one suffering this...natural human response.

He was suddenly back on the balcony the night before, Sadie's energy tangling with his, the stars shining in her eyes. Gravity, attraction, the heady pull of mutual intrigue, of the thrill of discovery drawing them together.

He was not unduly attracted to his old friend's runaway bride. It was simple science.

And yet he turned off the hot water and stuck his head under the cold until it began to burn.

When he'd punished himself enough, Will turned off the water, shaking off the chilly droplets. And stilled. Listening.

He'd heard something. A knock at the front door?

Hugo.

He reached for a towel to find the nearest towel rail empty. A quick glance found Sadie's towel flopped over the side of the bath.

Upon a thorough search he couldn't find another. So, grabbing her towel, he rubbed himself down, straining to hear voices. But the room seemed quiet.

"Sadie?" he called, his voice echoing in the small, steamy room. No response.

There. The front door opening. And closing.

"Dammit. Sadie!"

He couldn't seem to get himself dry. Because

the towel was damp. Redolent with the scent of honeysuckle.

"Saaadiiie!"

The bathroom door swung open and with the rush of clear air came Sadie. "What's wrong? Are you okay?"

Will swept the towel around his waist, clamping it together with one fierce hand at his hip. "Hell, Sadie!"

"What?" she said, swallowing a yawn. "You were the one bellowing my name."

Her hair was crushed against one side of her head where it had dried while she was sleeping. A crease from her pillow lined her cheek. Thankfully she was now wearing her dressing gown, though it sat twisted, half falling off one shoulder. When she absently tugged the sash tight it made no difference.

"I thought maybe you'd slipped, or…something." Her words faded as she seemed to realise his state of undress.

Under her unchecked gaze, Will felt the water dripping off his hair and rolling over his shoulders. His skin felt tight, and sensitive. Even with the heat of the shower still filling the room, goosebumps sprang up over his arms. When he felt other parts of himself beginning to stir he gathered the towel more tightly and growled, "Sadie."

She blinked. Slowly. Then she swallowed. Her next breath in was long and slow. Then her eyes rose to his. "Hmm? What? No? Wait... What on earth...?"

She took a full step towards him. Close enough that he saw the genuine worry in her eyes, the constellation of slightly darker freckles on her left cheek. Close enough that her hand hovered an inch from his chest.

She reached a hand towards his chest. Will clenched all over. Now what was she playing at?

Then she asked, "Is that a bruise?"

Will looked down to find a dark variegated stripe angling across his chest. He lifted a hand and ran it over the contusion. Thinking back, he came to a likely conclusion.

"I slammed on my brakes," he said, his voice rusty. "My seatbelt did its job."

Her eyes whipped to his. Energy crackled through the fog, the level fit to reach the back of a large theatre. "That's happened when you stopped for *me*? Does it hurt?"

She lifted her hand again, and this time he knew she was set to touch him.

Will caught her an inch from ground zero, holding her hand at bay. Her skin was cool against his. His thumb rested on her wrist, picking up the scattered throb of her pulse. Or perhaps it was his own.

Her pupils were huge and dark. Her cheeks high with colour and her breath no longer at ease.

Gravity. Attraction. Intrigue. Discovery.

"I'm fine." Will pressed his hand towards her before letting go. Then he turned and dug about inside his bag. Needing a break from those eyes. "Who was at the door?"

"The door?"

"The reason I called your name. I heard a knock."

"Right. Yes. I thought it might be Hugo… Alas. When I checked no one was there. But there was a gift basket left outside. Decorated in little love hearts for the honeymoon suite, no less."

Will gripped the edges of his bag. He was not a praying man, but in that moment he understood the impulse.

"Thank goodness, right? Because I'm starving."

Starving. Will's belly felt empty and his head a little light. A man his size couldn't live on adrenaline and chocolate-covered ginger alone. Food would help. It would alleviate the pangs. And he could recalibrate from there.

Oblivious to his internal bargaining, Sadie went on, "There's champagne, strawberries, chocolate, almonds, Vallemontian ginger. Some crackers and crisps. Even a tub of honey. I call the ginger."

"All yours," he managed, contemplating the veritable cornucopia of aphrodisiacs. "I don't have much of a sweet tooth."

"What a shock."

He looked up then. To find her gaze was on his chest once more. Not the scar—the rest. He could have told himself the aspiration in her gaze was all due to the food talk, but what would be the point?

Clearly a cold shower and rationalisation weren't going to do the trick.

He'd been on the back foot since this entire escapade began—a feeling he was neither used to nor welcomed.

Enough was enough. It was time to take charge.

He turned, reached into his bag, grabbed the

tracksuit she'd worn the day before and threw it at her.

She caught it. "What's this for?"

"Put it on. It'll be warmer than what you're wearing. And it's a grey old day out there."

"Thanks. That's really nice of you."

It was completely self-serving. "Was there something else?"

"No, but… I was just thinking about what the gift basket fairies might leave next? A collection of sonnets? Some massage oils? There's no TV so I guess that rules out—"

"Sadie."

"Yes, Will?"

"Get out."

"Yes, Will." She spun on her heel, all but scurrying from the room, closing the door with a loud snick.

That left Will to dress in the only clean clothes he had remaining—jeans and a black cashmere sweater.

He wiped his face, hung up his towel and tidied away his toiletries. He left no trace of himself behind.

And prayed when he checked his phone again Hugo would have sent word.

* * *

Will was back at the couch, repacking his bag for the tenth time that day, clearly wanting to be ready to go the moment she was off his hands. While Sadie—after living off strawberries, chocolate and champagne all day—felt super-twitchy and a little claustrophobic.

"Bored, bored, *bored*," she chanted under her breath.

Will turned, jaw tight, brow furrowed as if she'd interrupted him doing something terribly important. "Did you say something?"

"Nope. Maybe. I'm bored."

Will gave her a look. "Why don't you tidy up a little?"

"Nah."

"You are clearly used to having a maid."

"Are you kidding? My mother *is* the maid. At the palace. So was I, at times." She shuddered. "When Hugo was away ditching school with you, I begged Marguerite to put me to work. I helped look after the smaller royals—teaching them to clean up after themselves, to make their beds, to cook easy meals. Have you ever had to clean up the same Lego day after day after day?"

His blank look gave him away.

"That's right, you had a butler. Well, if you spend enough time cleaning up that stuff, one day you wake up and think, what's the point?"

"I never cleaned up my own Lego, Ms Gray, because my grandmother was rather old-fashioned when it came to the raising of children and did not believe in frivolous toys. That said, if the zombie apocalypse ever comes I'll be able to fence myself to freedom."

He went back to packing and she poked her tongue out at his back. Then she spun, held out fake pistols and muttered, "This room ain't big enough for the both of us."

"You definitely said something that time."

She blew invisible smoke from the top of a finger before sticking it back in her imaginary holster.

Things couldn't go on like this. This constant tension was messing with her equilibrium.

Like out on the balcony the night before— there'd been a moment when the wintry air had turned thick and steamy, when she'd looked into Will's dark eyes and seen something. Seen *him*. It had felt intimate, and thrilling, and terrifying. It was the kind of moment where something might have happened. The kind of something you couldn't take back.

And then in the bathroom this morning…she'd woken with a fright to the sound of his voice, the grit as he'd called her name. It hadn't occurred to her she might walk in on him half-dressed. Make that quarter-dressed. It had been too early in the morning to react sensibly to so much man. And how close had she come to feeling the guy up? He'd had to physically stop her from running her hand down his hard, muscular, naked—

Sadie sucked in a breath and shook her head.

Hugo had been right. Making friends with Will had to be better than…whatever was going on between them now.

She lifted her chin, manufactured a blinding smile and said, "So, Will, do you have a girlfriend waiting for you back in…wherever it is you're from?"

Wow. Excellent sentence-making skills, Sadie. Had she left her renowned charm in her "other" dress too? Apparently so, because Will wasn't charmed.

He kept on folding, waiting until everything was precise and in its place before deigning to reply. "No," he said. "And I was born in London."

No surprise. Grey, damp, so much snarling traffic they all but outlawed it, London was the polar opposite to the wide open, verdant green that was Vallemont. Though Hugo had taken her there for her eighteenth birthday, to see *The Tempest* in the West End, and that had been phenomenal.

Huh. Funny that Hugo hadn't made the effort to get in touch with Will, then, either. So whatever had happened between them was already in play. She'd get to that. But first:

"Really? No saucy smart girl with a lab coat, glasses and big brain to go home to?"

He gave her a sideways glance, still not giving an inch. And she knew there was no point even trying. He was just too… Will. He seemed to respond best to cool, clinical honesty.

Oh, well, here goes. "Come on, Will. Give me something. I'm drowning here."

"And what exactly do you mean by *something*?"

His deep, gravelly voice did things to her spine. Zappy, tingly things. She decided that was a little too much honesty and kept it to herself. "A little light small talk to while away the hours might be nice."

"Small talk?"

"Sure, why not?"

"Because it's asinine."

"Asinine? There you go. Something juicy for me to chew on." She took a deep breath and once again put on her best cowboy voice. *"Now, who do you think you are, calling me asinine?"*

He blinked. "I didn't. I said *small talk* was—"

She flapped a hand at him before plopping down on his couch, one foot under her backside, the other knee hooked up on the seat. Then she smacked the cushion, requesting he join her. "Sit. Let's get to know one another better. We might be here for days, after all. We might be here for ever."

Will lost a little colour at that last prediction.

"Sit. I dare you."

The colour returned.

He sat. The couch seemed to shrink, leaving her bent knee mere inches from his. But she held her ground. *All good here! My physical nearness to you is not a problem at my end!*

"So, where were we? No girlfriend. Great. I mean…fine. Okay. Glad we have that sorted." Then, because champagne and chocolate and boredom and…some new level of sadomasochism seemed to have taken her over, "But you do like girls, right?"

A slightly raised eyebrow and a flicker of his dimple was his only response.

"So, you *like* girls but you don't *have* a girl. Got it. I'm assuming it's that you're simply between girls and not because you're as much of a relationship screw-upper as I am."

His only response to her eventual silence was a look; dark and broody and gorgeous. Did she just say gorgeous? Only inside her head this time, which was okay. Except it wasn't even slightly okay!

Maybe it was some kind of Stockholm Syndrome. He'd practically kidnapped her, after all, and dragged her off to an actual tower, where he was keeping her hostage... Who knew what he had in mind for her?

Sadie wriggled on the seat, trying to shake off the tingle in her spine that didn't seem to want to go away. While also trying desperately not to let her knee touch his, because every time they touched, every time she bumped into him in the kitchen, or shuffled past him on the balcony, or passed him a cup of tea there was this spark, and warmth, and fast-spreading heat, and...

Will was still looking at her. His gaze locked on to her, not letting go. She could feel her heart rate speeding up and was getting that fuzzy feeling at the back of her skull. Like when a man was about to…

"My work is very important to me," said Will, thankfully cutting off her train of thought before it got away from her completely. "More than important. It's critical. It's also not conducive to long-term relationships."

She swallowed, hard, before managing, "How's that?"

"I work a great deal. I travel often. My plans change daily. I have a place in the Americas and Scandinavia as well as London, but my mail forwards to my assistant in Wisconsin. My publisher is in New York. The stars are always out somewhere in the world and so can I be too."

"Doctors work a lot. Firefighters too. Soccer players travel constantly. Many manage to settle down, have families." She could have just said, *That's nice.* Why was she pushing this?

"Ask those families if they'd prefer to have their partners and parents home more. I believe you'll get an unequivocal yes."

"So your singlehood is benevolent."

"Entirely." The way he said it, with a hint of humour in that whisky-rough voice of his, hit a spot deep down inside. Echoing. Reverberating. Before making itself at home.

"Well, good for you."

He nodded. The best she could manage was a toothless smile. Then, before she even felt the words coming, she said, "You must have questions."

Will's eyebrow twitched. "Many. Though they usually bend towards the esoteric—why are we here, how did we get here, what might happen next?"

"I meant about me…and Hugo."

Will went straight into his statue impersonation. Not moving, not breathing, not giving anything away. He was very good at it.

"No? Then let's start smaller. How about what's my favourite colour? Do I prefer ice cream or sorbet? What did I want to be when I—?"

"How long were you together?"

"Together? You mean Hugo and me? Hugo and I were never *together.*"

The guy could win a statue competition, hands down.

"We were the closest of friends since we were tiny tots. He'd pull me around in his little red wagon when he was three and drive me around in his big red Maserati when he was eighteen. And, because it never failed to bring a smile to someone's face, I'd declare to anyone who would listen that one day I was going to marry him."

"But you didn't mean it."

Sadie's breath caught. He'd known her a day and he got her. Those who'd known her a lifetime didn't have a clue.

She dragged her gaze away, the break of eyecontact a blessed relief. "Sure, we kissed a couple of times over the years—spin the bottle, three minutes in heaven, that kind of thing—in case it actually worked. But it never did. Not the way it should. It was to be a marriage of convenience. Separate quarters. Separate beds—"

Now Will moved, holding up a hand. "I know what a marriage of convenience means."

"Okay."

"But what I don't understand is why. Why get married at all?"

It was entirely her fault, but now they were moving into territories she wasn't comfortable talking about. It wasn't just her story to tell after all.

With a smile she said, "You've met the guy, right?"

"Several times. Wouldn't marry him, though."

"If you remember, neither would I."

Will shot her a look. Intense, intrigued. A life lived in the public eye, and she'd never felt quite so much as if she was under a microscope as she did now. Then, "Wait. Are you in some kind of trouble? Is that why he agreed to marry you?"

"Wow. You make him sound so gallant, deigning to stoop to—"

"*Sadie.*"

"No," she allowed. "Not in the way you mean."

"Then in what way?"

She wondered if Will had a clue that he'd suddenly sat up taller—shoulders back, fists braced on his thighs as if preparing to take on the as yet unknown trouble that had her in its thrall.

While she was trying so hard to appear cool and unaffected, it unglued her. He unglued her. Every time he went all gruff and protective on her behalf.

In the short time they'd been thrown together, he'd managed to see through her plucky façade to the truth. Her truth. In a way no one else had ever managed. She wondered now if anyone else had even bothered to try.

"Stop it," she said, her voice raspy. Her hands

gripping one another in her lap, hanging on for dear life.

"Stop what? I didn't say a word."

She licked her lips. "But you were thinking it. I can see it. All those big, heroic, take-over thoughts whipping around inside that ginormous brain of yours. Synapses firing at supersonic speed, sparking lights in your baby blues."

"Baby *what*?"

She waggled a hand towards his face. "Your eyes. Why, do you have something else blue on your person that I don't know about? Inner nostrils? Belly-button lint? No, I would have seen it when you called me into the bathroom this morning. And what was that really all about? You couldn't have pulled on some clothes beforehand?"

Sadie's gaze dropped to Will's chest, saliva actually pooling in her mouth as she remembered.

"Wasn't it Shakespeare who had something to say about a lady protesting too much?"

She coughed out a laugh as her eyes swung back to his. So intense, so clever, so unrelenting. "Seriously? This is the conversation you want to be having?"

When he didn't demur, she knew she had to get

out of there. But where? The steamy bathroom and her memories of Will half-naked? The balcony, where anyone could see her? With its palace view and memories of looking at the stars with Will? Maybe it was time to run again. At least she was wearing a tracksuit this time...

She made to stand, but as soon as her foot hit the floor she realised it had gone numb. Unable to take her weight, it collapsed and with a *whoop* she toppled.

Will reached out and caught her with all her gangly limbs and flailing panic. He braced, taking the worst of the impact as they landed in a heap on the couch. A telling *oomph* shot from his lungs as her knee jabbed him in the thigh, her elbow slamming him right in the solar plexus.

As she waited for her own aches and pains to show themselves, she couldn't feel anything bar the fact her body was all up against Will's. She felt as if she had a hundred senses, not the normal five. Each one focused on hard muscle, strong arms, warm, masculine scent.

"Sadie," he said. "Sadie, are you hurt?"

She squeezed her eyes shut and shook her head.

"Are you sure? Because you're shaking."

Trembling. She was trembling. Emotion, adrenaline, lust, fear, exhaustion, confusion—all were rolling through her in satiny, liquid waves.

Will reached up to brush her hair from her face, tucking it behind her ear.

Her eyes flickered open in surprise and landed on his.

He should have let his hand drop then. They both knew it. Instead his thumb lingered, just a moment, brushing over the high sweep of her cheek. Following the sweet, warm rush of heat rising in her face.

The move was so unexpected, so gentle, so *tender*, she couldn't handle it.

She shifted, and he grimaced. Not with agony. She knew the way a woman knew. He was bracing himself against the slide of her body against his.

Even before Will's hand moved around her back, sliding up her ribs, into her hair, he said, "Stop. Moving."

"Okay." She licked her lips. "But I have to move eventually."

"Just not yet."

When he breathed she felt it against her mouth, her neck, everywhere. It was a rush. A terrible, wonderful, overwhelming rush, asking too much, not asking for enough.

She could not want this man. Not the way her body was trying to tell her she did. He was Hugo's friend. A man Hugo had trusted to be on her side, meaning that Hugo thought Will was on his side.

If this whole debacle had taught her anything, surely it was to stop thinking she could make it work with men she couldn't have.

Her acting coach in New York had adored the way she had looked up to him. The estimable Prince of Vallemont adored her as a friend. And insular, unreachable, closed-off Dr Will Darcy...

There was no adoration here. Only attraction. Compulsion. And a sweet, raw, formidable urge to pack away her need to be liked and simply get real.

"Will," she said, her voice soft, her heart aching with regret.

"Mmm?"

"I'm sorry you got caught up in all this. But I'm also not sorry at all."

The look in his eyes was tragic. Tortured.

Then he opened his mouth to speak—

But Sadie never got to find out what he'd been about to say next because just then someone knocked on the door.

CHAPTER SEVEN

FEELING AS IF he'd swallowed a lead balloon, Will said, "Expecting anyone?"

Sadie shook her head, her hair sliding over his collarbone like silk. Her next breath in she was shifting her body over his, her next breath out she seemed to melt over him like chocolate on a summer's day.

Then she blinked, her oceanic eyes widening. "Well, apart from whoever Hugo plans on sending in to whisk me away." She swallowed. "Has he sent word?"

"Nothing since yesterday."

The knock came again. Not the dainty taps that had heralded the gift basket but harder, more insistent, like a secret code.

Then, even though he was not in the right frame of mind, or body for that matter, to talk to anyone, Will found some reserve of inner strength in order to lift her bodily away, place her back in the chair and heave himself to standing.

He took a few moments to bring himself back under some semblance of control before he moved to the door and looked through the peephole.

What he saw made him take a literal step back. As time contracted, and his gut squeezed tight, he considered ignoring the knock. The moment passed, as moments tended to do. And good sense returned. *This* was what he wanted. This was what he'd been waiting for.

"This'll be cosy," he muttered, widening the door.

And there stood Hugo.

Taller than Will, just. Lines fanning out from the edges of his eyes where there'd been none before. A short dark beard now covered his jaw, but the chronic wealth and the resplendent royal Vallemontian bloodline was evident in every cell. With the antiquated newspaper rolled up under one arm, the way the collar of his button-down shirt was turned up at the neck it was simply so particularly Hugo, Will burst into laughter.

And reached out a hand.

Hugo's face split into a matching grin as he shook it. "Good to see you too, my friend."

Hugo glanced back towards the neckless, black-clad man-mountain with the bald head and the frown standing guard at the end of the hall. "I'll message when we're done."

The man-mountain nodded and hulked down the hall.

Only then did Hugo step into the breach to wrap Will in a manly hug. Double back-slap and all. And just like that the years between them faded to nothing.

"Hugo?"

Sadie's voice cut through and both men turned to face the room.

"Oh, my God! Oh, my God!" Like the Doppler effect, Sadie's voice lifted and grew as she vaulted over the back of the couch and ran towards them, her hair flying behind her.

Hugo had about half a second to drop his newspaper and the overnight bag he'd had slung over his shoulder before she leapt into his arms. Like a teddy bear with Velcro hands, she buried her face in his neck. Hugo's eyes squeezed closed, his voice rough even though muffled by her hair.

"Leo."

"What the heck are you doing here, you great fool? I assumed you'd send a lackey. Or maybe just a car. You didn't have to come."

"Of course I did."

Imagining them together was one thing. Theorising why it made little sense was another. Watching them, like this, their affection a real, live, pulsing thing, Will gripped the door handle so hard the thing creaked in protest. "Perhaps we ought to move this reunion inside."

Hugo's eyes found Will; filled with a level of understanding Will knew the man couldn't possibly have. Then he nodded his agreement and walked inside with Sadie still attached like a limpet.

Will shut the door, perhaps a tad harder than necessary.

At the sound, Sadie lifted her head. She tapped Hugo on the back and when he placed her on the ground she peeled herself away. "I can't believe you're actually here."

"Yet here I am."

"Excellent. This is just excellent." She glanced at Will, her cheeks now pinking like crazy.

And what Will thought was, *She's about to give us away entirely.* Except there was nothing tangible to give away. Only a little gravitational theory. And a whole lot of misplaced heat energy.

It didn't matter now. Hugo was here. Will's job

was done. It was time for him to bow out. To get on a plane. To get back to work.

"Come in!" said Sadie. "Tell me everything. No, not everything. I might need a little Dutch courage before we get to that."

Hugo smiled as Sadie took him by the arm, but the look in his eyes showed he was pensive.

And from one breath to the next Will knew he wasn't going anywhere. Not just yet.

Not that he didn't trust Hugo, but the Prince's interests were divided. Naturally so. He had his own legacy, his own future to consider. He also had an entire royal house breathing down his neck. Will had been charged with keeping Sadie safe, so he'd stick around a little longer and finish the job properly.

He moved the overnight bag—Sadie's by the looks of it—to the door and picked up the newspaper Hugo had dropped, giving the front page a quick glance. The non-wedding was the headliner. No surprise there.

When he looked up, Will noticed Sadie had bypassed the nearest couch to sit Hugo on the other. The one Will *hadn't* slept on. The one on which they had not just been wrapped up in one another...

Will cleared his throat. When Hugo looked over he pointed to the newspaper, asking, "Any concern with this lot on your way here?"

"We were careful."

"Be grateful you're not British," said Will. "Or they'd be camped out on the roof, climbing the trellis, crawling out of the toilet bowl by now."

"I'm grateful of that each and every day."

Old jokes. Old friendship. All new tension in the air as Sadie sat on the edge of the couch, leg jiggling, nibbling at her bottom lip, energy levels spiking.

"How long have you and the man in black been special friends?" Will asked.

Hugo's cheek twitched. "Since an attempt was made on my uncle's life a year ago. While he was picnicking with Princess Marguerite and the twins."

That was half the Vallemontian succession plan right there. Another tragic event would have brought Hugo within sight of the throne. "I hadn't heard."

"It was kept quiet."

"Were they all right?"

"Shaken up. But unharmed." Hugo sent Sadie a comforting wink. "Against my express wishes,

Prospero turned up the next day. I have offered him gainful employment in any number of positions since, and yet I can't shake the guy."

"It must be a constant struggle, being so beloved."

"And yet I never let the hardship get to me."

Sadie laughed. Quieted. Laughed again. "Who the hell are you two and what have you done with Hugo and Will?"

Hugo gave her a pat on the knee. Chummy. Friendly. "Don't tell anyone but all men are teenaged boys in the bodies of grown-ups. Now, I'd kill for a glass of water."

Sadie sprang out of the seat. "I can do better than that. Will, you start the fire. Hugo, you tidy the coffee table. I'm sure I saw designer beers in the bottom of the fridge."

Will watched her bounce into the kitchen. "Where's the, *Please, Your Majesty*?"

"Ask her," said Hugo. "I dare you."

"Hey, Sadie?" Will called.

Sadie pulled her head out of the fridge. "Mmm?"

"I hid some cheese and crackers in the pantry so we wouldn't starve."

"Perfect!"

Hugo laughed under his breath. "Coward."

Will crouched to pick out kindling and a good-sized log. "At least she gave me the manly job. She has you on tidying duty."

"Fair point. Leo?" Hugo called.

"Mm hmm."

"Do I have to tidy?"

"It builds character."

"Fine," Hugo mumbled, before making space on the coffee table.

Leo? Will thought. Oh my god. *Leo*.

Will had quietly wondered why he couldn't remember Hugo mentioning Sadie while at school, if they'd known one another as long as she'd intimated. But flashes came back to him now. Hugo talking about *Leo's* terrible taste in music. Rock climbing with *Leo*. Plans to hit Oktoberfest with *Leo*.

Hugo had spoken as if talking about a great mate. Not even the slightest hint of romance. While the stories had been about Mercedes Gray *Leo*nine, naturally Will had thought "Leo" was a boy.

Giving in to a sudden urge to whistle a happy tune, Will set to starting a fire. Out of the corner of his eye he saw Sadie with a packet of crackers hanging from her teeth, cheese hooked into her elbow and a knife between two knuckles, three beers in one hand. Barefoot, hair cascading over her shoulder, her small frame swamped by his tracksuit.

Either Hugo had become less observant over the years or he was holding off from passing comment on the story behind the outfit. Odds were the latter; the question was *why*.

When Will stood it was to find Hugo leaning back in the chair, hands behind his head, looking content.

"Here you go, big guy," said Sadie.

Hugo held out a hand and Sadie dutifully handed him a beer. "Much appreciated."

Then Sadie placed a hand on Hugo's knee as she leant over his legs to hand a beer to Will. "And one for you."

He took it with a nod.

She smiled quickly and pink heat flushed her cheeks again. He felt it too. The echo of a pulsing red haze that had come over him on the couch; her soft body flush against his, her hair sweeping against his neck.

Will tipped his drink towards her. She took a

big swig of hers, then dumped the rest of the picnic on the coffee table.

"S'cuse," she said, nudging her way past Hugo's legs, taking a quick survey of the space and choosing a piece of floor in between them. "Tell me, in gory detail, how is it out there?"

"I'd say it's pretty mild for this late in the year."

"Jeans and jumper weather?" Will asked.

Hugo nodded. "I'd take a coat, just in case."

"Boys," Sadie chastised, shooting each of them a glare. "This is a war meeting. Not a party. Now, what do I need to do from here? How can I help mitigate the damage? For you. Your family. My mother—"

"Your mother is fine," said Hugo. "In fact…"

"In fact what?"

"She handed in her resignation."

"She *what*?"

"Apparently she told Marguerite she has been wanting to retire for years. She has quite the nest egg, an eye on a small cottage in the village near your school and a penchant to travel."

"Why didn't she say anything to me?"

"She didn't want to disappoint you."

"Disappoint *me*? But the entire reason I agreed to marry you was so that she could stay on after she stops working. I mean, *part* of the reason, because, well, I'd been told there'd be a tiara in it for me. A really big one. And you are, of course, you."

Hugo waved an understanding hand her way.

But Will realised he'd stopped with his beer halfway to his mouth. "Can we rewind just a second?"

Hugo and Sadie glanced his way—expressions of barely restrained patience exactly the same.

"Did I just hear that you were marrying this lug so your mother could live in the palace after she retires?"

Sadie answered, "That was a deciding factor. Yes."

Will sat forward, and turned on Hugo. "And why the hell were you marrying her?"

"Whoa," said Sadie. "A tad too effusive in your level of disbelief there, cowboy."

Hugo laughed. "He makes a fair point. I am ridiculously eligible."

Sadie batted her lashes at Hugo. "And rich."

"And devilishly handsome."

Sadie ran a hand through her hair; most of it settled back into place but some hooked on the hood of Will's track top. Light from the fire inside sparked off the russet tones like flares from the sun. It would take nothing to unhook it for her, to let it run through his fingers.

Nothing but his dignity.

Will's voice was a growl. "Get a room already."

Hugo looked around. "I could say we already have one, but this has a little too much chintz for my taste."

Will let his half-drunk beer drop to the coffee table and rubbed a hand over his chin as he attempted to sort the actual evidence from the white noise, only to find he'd forgotten to shave yet again. Unlike him.

He ran his hands through his hair instead, as if that might massage his brain into gear, and said, "The attempt on Sovereign Prince Reynaldo and his family—it was more of a near thing than you made out. If it had been a success, you would have been damn near the front of the succession line. Reynaldo is a serious ruler. A serious man. That realisation had him rethink the leeway you've enjoyed since your father passed. He made you an offer. Or a threat."

"Wow," said Sadie. "You're good."

Hugo's smile was flat. "Since my mother is not of royal blood, and Australian-born, her position here is precarious. Especially now that she has remarried—a Frenchman, and a commoner no less. The law is clear: without my father she lives at the palace at the grace of the family until I come of age."

"At…?"

"Three and thirty."

"Next year. And then?"

"If I marry she may stay. If not…"

"I see."

"Do you?"

"She must leave the palace."

"Without citizenship, without naturalisation, without a partner from Vallemont to sponsor her, my mother would be forced to leave the country."

Will coughed out a laugh. It was laughable. Archaic. Nonsensical. And by the twin expressions looking back at him, true. And then he was laughing no more. "So he was marrying you for real estate and you were marrying for the sake of…" He looked to Sadie. "What? Security?"

"Don't knock it. Security is pretty sought after. Especially for those who don't have it."

Hugo offered up a hand for a high five.

"So you were both being altruistic to the point of sadomasochism?" Will was right to stay a little longer. He ran a hand through his hair, tugging at the ends. "You're cracked. The both of you."

"And you're so very British," said Hugo.

"Isn't he?" Sadie agreed. Then, to Will, "Our sensibilities are not as draconian as yours. It is normal for Vallemontians to openly marry for any number of reasons: business, property, partnership, companionship. Even— shock, horror— for true love."

Hugo stopped her there. "Don't bother, Leo. They say no man is an island, but even before he discovered the stars Will was always a planet."

"Hugo," Sadie chastised.

But Will stayed her with a smile. "I was trying to remember why we hadn't seen one another in an age, but now it's all come back to me."

Only it hadn't. Not until that moment. Somehow he'd been so caught up in protecting Sadie— from herself, it turned out—he'd not seen Hugo and thought *Clair*.

From the flash of pain in the Prince's eyes Clair's ghost was now on his mind as well.

"What?" said Sadie. "What just happened there? What am I missing?"

But words were not possible. Will's throat had closed up. The edges of his vision blurring. Clair was not something he spoke of. In fact, he hadn't spoken to anyone who'd actually known her in years. It was too brittle. Too terrible. The loss of her was as much a part of him as his ribs.

But Hugo, it turned out, was not so bound. "Do you remember my friend Clair?"

Sadie looked at Hugo and back to Will. "Clair. You mean from the high school near yours? Of course. She came to stay that summer."

"Clair was Will's twin sister."

Will had seen Sadie shaken, seen her scared and he'd seen her cry. He'd seen her eyes warm and melt. But he had not, until that moment, seen her focus, the cessation of energy coming from her position like a sudden black hole.

Then she said, "You're *Clair's* brother. The one who was meant to come to Vallemont that summer, but couldn't because you…"

"I broke my leg."

She clicked her fingers at him. "Yes! From what I remember Hugo had quite the crush on young Clair. Followed her around like a puppy. I might have even been a mite jealous—because I hadn't had him to myself for months—if not for the fact I had a bit of a girl crush on her too. She taught herself to play the guitar, remember, Hugo? From nothing. And she was obsessed with Marguerite's accent. She had the impression down pat. She was rather too taken with Ibsen to truly be trusted. But she was fun. And you say you're her twin? Will wonders never cease?"

On her saunter down memory lane Sadie was clearly missing the undercurrents. For Hugo had gone deadly quiet, while Will was eating up her every word. He was swimming in visions of Clair laughing, creating, keeping the palace in thrall. Filling in gaps of the time he'd missed. He'd spent so long blaming Hugo for stealing those last days, when the truth was Will's old friend had given her a wonderfully rich final summer.

It wasn't Clair's death that had ripped their friendship apart. It was Will's anger. His grief. The fact that he'd been eviscerated. The next couple of years were a wretched blur. Until he woke up again in that astronomy lecture, and never looked back.

Never truly faced his grief. Never truly let go.

"Whatever did happen to Clair?" Sadie asked. "Why isn't she here? Too heartbroken over the one that got away?"

Will's gaze shot to Hugo to find the Prince looking deep into his beer. *Come on, Hugo, give me a hand here.* Hugo took a long, slow swig, but refused to look Will's way.

It seemed Will would have to find the words after all. "She fell ill."

"Oh, poor thing."

"No… I mean, years ago. Clair died not long after that summer."

Sadie's hand went to her mouth as she rose to her knees, her gaze zapping between the men. "No. I can't believe it."

Will nodded.

"I'm so sorry, Will, I had no idea. And there I was, fluffing on about ridiculous impressions and how gaga we were over her."

"It's okay," Will said, surprised to find he meant it. "It was actually good to hear. To think of her having a good time."

Sadie looked into his eyes, deep, searching, demanding honesty. "How did she die?"

"Sadie," said Hugo, speaking up for the first time.

"If Will doesn't want to talk about it he'll tell me. You on the other hand don't get to weigh in here because this is all news to me and that is your fault. What happened?"

Will twisted his knuckles, easing out the tension, and soon found himself saying, "It started with memory loss. Personality changes. Depression. You met her, she was…sunny. When we'd all gone back to school I started receiving letters in which she sounded anxious, aggrieved. I figured she must have fought with Hugo even though he denied it. I asked my school to allow me to check in. As a known truant they refused me, so I begged my grandmother to intervene. My grandmother was not moved. It wasn't until the first seizure that anyone else thought anything was wrong. By the time they had Clair in hospital her speech was impaired, her balance dysfunctional. Pneumonia hit three weeks later. And then she was gone." Will's voice didn't feel like his own. It felt a hundred years old. "I had not seen her in person since I broke my leg."

"Since Vallemont?"

"That's right." Out of the corner of his eye Will saw Hugo shift in his seat.

"Is it hereditary?" Sadie asked.

A note of concern in her voice had Will lifting his eyes. "No. It was the spontaneous misfolding of a protein. Nothing anyone could have done."

"So, you're okay?"

"I'm okay."

"Okay, then." Her eyes caught the reflection of the fire as she turned on Hugo. "Alessandro Hugo Giordano, what were you thinking in not telling me?"

Hugo refused to answer and Sadie rocked back onto her feet and stood. "I'm sorry to hear about your sister, Will. But I can't look at him right now. I need a moment."

And with a withering look sent Hugo's way, she went. The creak of the French windows opening was followed by a stream of chilly air.

"That went well," said the Prince.

"Oh, hello," said Will, grabbing his beer once more. "You've been so quiet I'd forgotten you were here."

"Nowhere else in the world I'd rather be."

"I vote for the Bahamas."

Hugo raised his beer. Will gave it a clink. And together they drank. Unlike the beers they'd secreted during not-so-secret parties their American dorm-mate used to host in his room after hours, this felt more like a wake. A toast. To Clair.

The girl they'd both loved. The girl they both missed. And just like that Will felt as if a weight that had rested on his shoulders for years lifted.

Hugo shifted. Cleared his throat. And changed the subject. "So, Will, how's life been treating you these last million years?"

"Can't complain."

"My mother showed me an article about you in a magazine a month or so back. Which one was it?"

"Time? New Yorker? American Scientist?" He could have named dozens.

Hugo clicked his fingers. *"Top Twenty: sexiest living scientists* issue. I particularly liked the 'living' addendum. Clearly if they'd opened up the field to intellectuals of eras past you wouldn't have stood a chance."

Will's laughter now came without restraint. No one in his life today had known him before he was someone. Before the university awards, the publishing deal, the infamy in his field. No one in his life had known him as a troubled kid with an incorrigible twin sister he'd loved more than anything.

But he was that kid. He'd had that sister. Pressing it deep down inside, never to be talked about, had not made it go away. Did not make it hurt any less. It only made it fester.

Time to let in a little sunshine. Time to heal.

"So how do you like my Leo?" Hugo asked.

And as if he couldn't stop himself now, Will laughed again. "I like her just fine."

"Really? Because every time you look at her you roll your shoulders as if trying to shake her off. She's under your skin, my friend."

Will's gaze slid to the open French window. Like a moth to the flame. "Stick anyone in a room with her for twenty-four hours and she'd get under their skin."

"And that's the truth. She had a hard beginning to things, you know. Father left her and her mother on the side of the road the day she was born."

Will ran a hand up the back of his neck. "Hell."

"Could have been. Marguerite found them and took them in. The entire country adopted her as their own. It would be difficult to find one's feet under so many watchful eyes. I've handled it by creating a life, a purpose, separate from the renown. She handled it by being the sweet, funny, happy, grateful kid she thought everyone expected her to be."

Hugo rested a finger over his mouth.

"She's the one person in my life I can trust to call me on my bullshit. And I care for her more than I care for anyone. But I also clearly misread her. What she must have suffered—to go through with my plan for this long and then run. I know she is determined to take the blame, but this is entirely my fault. She'll forgive me when she finally realises it—she's all heart. But I'm not sure I'll ever forgive myself."

Will knew Hugo wasn't looking for a response, merely a listening ear. So he listened. He heard. And he tried with all his might not to let it colour his feelings for Sadie. They were convoluted enough as it was without adding pathos to her tale. She had a sweet, determined kind of dauntlessness. But it was best to remember her as an unexpected variance in his life's path. And nothing more.

"Anyway." Hugo pulled himself to standing and Will did the same. "I'll just make a quick stop and then it's time for us to leave."

Hugo reached out a hand. Will took it.

The Prince tipped his head. "Thank you for stepping up in my stead, old friend. She couldn't have landed in better hands."

Will's gut clenched, looking for signs Hugo meant the words in a way other than how they appeared. But he seemed only grateful.

Will nodded. "I'm glad I could be of help."

Hugo let go, patted Will on the shoulder, then jogged towards the bathroom. The moment his friend was out of sight, Will turned his gaze east. Towards sunset. Towards night. Towards the stars.

Towards the open French window and goodbye.

Sadie looked up into the sky. The first stars had begun to twinkle high above her, the deep red sunset over the mountains masked the rest. The small village below was even quieter than the evening before. As if everyone had simply gone on with their lives.

She breathed in long and hard as her mind flipped through memories of Clair, her breath shaky as she let it go. It was silly really, feeling so bereft about a girl she'd known for a few weeks so long ago. She could barely even remember what she looked like apart from dark wavy hair. A quick smile. Bright, mischievous eyes.

When Hugo had come back from school at the end of that next year, and not mentioned her again, she'd assumed they had drifted apart. And, knowing Hugo as she did, she'd let it go. All the while he must have been in such pain.

And to think that warm, funny girl was cool, clever Will's sister. His twin sister, no less. How must losing her have affected him? He'd been, what? Sixteen? Seventeen?

Sadie felt swamped. Off kilter. As if everything she thought she knew about Will had shifted just a fraction to the right. Where there was a two-dimensional thorn in her side, now there was warmth, sorrow, angles, depth, adding rabid curiosity to what had been, up until that point, rabid physical attraction.

None of which mattered a jot.

Hugo was here.

She was leaving with him.

Will would…do whatever it was Will did with his time wherever in the world he did it. The fact that she couldn't quite imagine what that might look like made her feel even worse.

She gripped the railing hard. The air had turned so bitterly cold it felt as though it might even snow.

Her breath hitched before she even knew why. And she turned to find Will stepping over the threshold and onto the balcony.

She gave him a small smile. He gave her one back. Then he moved to stand beside her, his hands gripping the freezing cold railing mere inches from hers. But not touching. Things unsaid swirling about them like a storm.

"Time to go?" she asked.

Will nodded.

"But where?" she said. "That is the question."

"Home?"

"I'm not sure where that is any more."

"Not a bad thing in my experience. Where would you like to go now you have the chance?"

"I have no idea. I truly hadn't let myself think past yesterday. Not to the honeymoon, or to my new living quarters, or to how I was going to get my job back. I think, deep down, I was sure someone would call us out, that it would never actually happen." She shook her head. Old news. The future was now. "Anyway, I should... I was going to say pack, but I have nothing. No home, no prince, no job. Just me."

"Sounds like you have plenty."

At the note in Will's voice—husky and raw—Sadie's eyes swept to the man beside her. The dark curls, the strong face, those profoundly deep eyes—he looked like some Byronic hero. He looked...so beautifully tragic, her entire body began to unfurl. To reach for him. To ease his aches and pains. And, yes, her own.

How had she come to be so used to having him in her life? It had been a day and a half, for Pete's sake. How had she become so attuned to the subtlety of his movements, his expressions, his breaths? So responsive to the quiet questions in his eyes?

She closed herself back in, crossing both arms over her chest. "Thank you, Will. For the tracksuit, for the bed, for putting up with me."

"I won't say it's been my pleasure—"

She smiled, as she was meant to do.

"But it has been educational."

Sadie reached out, laid her hand on Will's arm. "From a smart guy like you I'll take that as a compliment."

"From a generous spirit like yours, I wouldn't expect anything different."

Sadie should have let go. Instead she stepped forward, tipped up onto her toes and pressed her lips to Will's cheek.

Even as it happened she knew she would never forget the scent of him—soap and heat and man. Or the warmth of his body, enveloping hers. The scrape of his stubble against her lips. Or the telling shiver that rocketed down his arm and into her hand. Like a perfect circuit.

When she pulled away, her heart was clanging in her chest. Breaths were difficult to come by. The intensity in his eyes was nothing like she'd felt in her entire life.

And once again the spell was broken by a knock at the door.

Shaking her head, literally, she landed back on her heels. Then she took a step towards the room. "Did Hugo go out?"

But Will put a hand over the door, protecting her. "No. Wait here."

She didn't wait, she followed. He might harbour a protective streak a mile wide, but she could look after herself. To find Hugo was already at the door, eye at the peephole.

He opened the door with a flourish to reveal Prospero filling the doorway.

"Prospero," said Hugo. "Excellent timing. We're ready to—"

The big man held out his phone. "Your Highness."

Hugo winced. "For the hundredth time, it's Hugo, please."

The big man's expression didn't falter. "Your Highness, you need to see this."

"Fine." Hugo took the phone, his expression blank. Until it wasn't. His brow furrowed, his mouth thinned. He seemed to grow out of his shoes until he looked for all the world a king. His voice was sharp as he demanded, "Where did you find this?"

"Internet alerts," said Prospero. "Any hint of a news article about you comes into my phone. I need to be prepared." The big man's throat worked ever so slightly, the only sign he was in any way concerned. "I blame myself. They must have followed us from the palace. I have failed you at the first sign of trouble. I will resign the moment I get you to safety."

Hugo gave him a look. "You're not quitting. I've only just got used to having you around. And it looks like I'm going to need you tonight."

When Will stepped forward, Sadie realised she'd been tucked in behind him, taking his protection for granted. She moved past him and tugged on Hugo's sleeve. "What is it? What's going on?"

Hugo glanced over her shoulder at Will.

Sadie took Hugo by his royal chin and forced

him to look at her. Out of the corner of her eye she saw Prospero move in. To the big bald man she said, "Back away." To Hugo, "And you. Tell me what's going on. Right now."

Hugo gave over his phone.

Sadie recognised the website. It was the kind that traded in online gossip, most of it made up. All salacious. Whatever their opinion on the wedding upset, no one would take it seriously, surely.

And then she saw the art.

There was Hugo walking into a building. Crumbling brick. Bougainvillaea. A swing sign with a tulip carved into the wood.

She looked up at Hugo. "That's you. Walking in here. This afternoon."

"Keep going."

Finger shaking now, she scanned down. Her hand moved to cover her mouth as she saw the worst of it.

More pictures. This time it was later, darker. The shots angled up at the Tower Room balcony. Some images weren't even in focus but every one of them was all too clear.

Picture after picture of Sadie and Will. Hands an inch apart as they held the railing. Looking into one another's eyes.

Sadie's throat tightened as she madly scanned through the lot. Thankfully the pictures stopped before she had taken Will by the arm. Leaned in. Kissed him.

Small mercy. For under each picture the banner read, "Prince Alessandro busts Lady Sadie with new lover in secret village pad."

She'd known the balcony wasn't secure. The entire village was spread out below with its houses and shops and bars. Will's self-sabotage theory grew roots and shoots and twisted around her like a creeping vine.

"Hugo, we were just talking." That was Will, looking over Sadie's shoulder as she slowly scrolled back.

"I know," said Hugo.

"I mean, it was right now. Just happened. Look at the clothes. The angle of the shadows—"

"Will, I know. I trust you weren't just romancing Leo on the balcony like something from one of her plays. It's okay."

Head swimming, tummy tumbling, Sadie shoved the phone at Hugo before it burned her hand, clueless as to whether to apologise or smack him.

She turned to Prospero, ready to flay him for

bringing the press here, but the big guy looked so desperately disgraced that in another place, another era, he might have popped an arsenic tablet and been done with it.

She looked around the room for answers. It really was a sweet room. If one had to get stuck somewhere for any length of time it was a wonderful choice. She'd miss it. Or maybe it was the simplicity. The time to do nothing but reflect on the life choices she'd made. The company...

It didn't matter. For now it was time to go.

Hugo broke into her reverie. "Will, what's your plan?"

"London."

"Take her with you."

In the gap left by Will's revealing silence, Sadie said, "Am I the *her* in this situation?"

Her eyes flickered between theirs. Hugo had gone full prince—looking down his nose imperiously, as if he was about to bestow a knighthood. While Will was pulling his statue move. These men...

"Will can't just take me with him. He works. He has a life." Sadie realised she wasn't sure what that entailed. Despite the intensity of the past couple of days, she didn't really know the man at all. "Tell him, Will."

But Will was watching Hugo, the two men having some kind of psychic Man Conversation of which she was no part.

Sadie looked to Prospero for help. "Prospero, tell them they're overreacting."

Anguish passed over Prospero's face. "Sorry, m'lady. But His Highness is right. The sooner you are gone, the easier it is for me to protect the Prince. It's best."

Sadie threw her hands in the air. "'It's best'? *It's best* is how we got into this mess in the first place!"

Knowing the barb was meant for him, Hugo finally looked at her. She took her chance. "If Will and I are seen together, leaving the country no less, those pictures will take on loaded meaning where right now there is nothing but two separate, uninvolved people on a balcony. Chatting. About…stuff."

Only she couldn't stop the strangely guilty warmth rising in her cheeks, because for her it had meant more than simply chatting. If Hugo noticed he didn't say, but something passed over his face, nevertheless. Ruefulness? Or maybe it was release.

Sadie turned on Will, getting desperate now. "Will. You say the word and we can put an end to this idea."

Will's gaze turned to Sadie. All deep soulful eyes and tight, ticking jaw. And he said, "It's fine."

"Wow, how to make a girl feel wanted."

A flash of fire lit the depths of his eyes, of *want*. It lit a twin fire in her belly, lower. Higher. All over. This was going to be a disaster.

"Don't you see you're off the hook? You're not my babysitter any more. You're not my bodyguard."

"Then what is he?" Hugo asked.

"He's… He's…" So many conflicting answers rushed to the front of Sadie's mind, none of which she could say out loud.

Hugo took her silence for acquiescence. "Exactly. It's done. Prospero?"

"I'm on it." And then the big man was off, striding down the hall.

Hugo shoved an overnight bag at her. "I had your mother pack for you, just in case you decided against coming home right away. Clothing, toothbrush, et cetera. A book. Your phone. Charger. And your passport."

Passport? She'd run out of excuses. Unless she wanted to be hunted in her own backyard, she had to go. It was best.

Will gathered his leather overnight bag and his battered silver case. *He'd* been packed, ready to go, from the moment they'd arrived. "Let's do this."

And then they were off. Hugo at the head, Sadie in the middle, Will at the rear.

"Breathe," Will murmured.

"Don't want to."

Then his hand slipped under her elbow and he walked beside her. "Do it anyway."

"Story of my life."

His rough laughter made her feel as if she'd stepped into a warm bath. The tingling in her toes diminished and her anxiety eased.

Striding down the hall, down the stairs and into Reception, they saw that Prospero had taken up residence with his back to the front door.

Janine of the ponytail was at the desk once more, watching Prospero like a hawk. When she looked up to see Will bearing down on her, her whole face brightened. "Why, hello! If it isn't the lovebirds from the honeymoon suite!"

Sadie blanched. Not that Janine would have noticed. Her eyes were now comically jumping from Will to Prospero to Hugo.

"Heading out?" Janine called. "It's cold out there—" Her voice came to a halt as her mouth dropped open into comical shock. "You're…him. You're the… Oh, my."

Hugo stepped up to the plate, blinding smile in place. "Prince Alessandro. Pleased to meet you. Is there, by any chance, a back entrance to this place? We seem to have collected some unsavoury hangers-on."

Janine, good girl that she was, did not need to be asked twice. She was out from behind the counter in a flash. "This way," she stage-whispered, tiptoeing dramatically.

Will, Hugo and Sadie followed, edging through the old kitchen, and out into an alleyway filled with limp bougainvillaea petals, bins and a half-dozen stray cats. As luck would have it they could see the bumper of Will's hire car out the other end.

To Will Hugo said, "Take care of her as if she

is your most precious possession. Take care of her as if she is family."

Will's nod was solemn.

"Thanks again, Will," said Hugo, shaking the other man's hand. "I owe you."

"You owe me nothing."

"Can you let Maman know?" asked Sadie.

"Of course." Hugo gave Sadie a quick bear hug. "Try not to cause too much trouble."

She laughed. "Way too late for that."

"Go. Now."

Will grabbed Sadie's bag from her shoulder and strode towards the car. Sadie followed, noting it had started to snow. Big, soft, romantic flakes that dissolved the second they hit skin.

Her feet ground to a halt as she neared the end of the alley, and moonlit hit her toes. "Just a second."

She ran back to Hugo, who was waiting in the darkness, delved deep into the zip pocket in the side of her track top and found the ring which was still attached to the garter. She gave it to Hugo.

He winced. "Maybe I ought to gift this thing to the twins and be done with it."

"Don't say that. You'll find someone one day.

Someone wonderful. Someone who adores you. Someone who doesn't cringe at the thought of kissing you. Someone who doesn't answer back all the time and isn't such a bad sport at board games as I am. Someone, maybe, a little like Clair."

A moment of torment crossed her old friend's face like a cloud passing the moon, and she wondered that she'd never noticed before.

Then he pulled himself free of it and gave her a smile. "Take care, Leo."

"You too, Hugo."

And with that, Sadie ran and hopped into the car. Or she tried, but her wedding dress was still smooshed into the footwell, her hairpiece sitting pathetically on top.

She hopped out of the car, dragged out the wedding stuff, went to the bin in the alleyway and threw it all away.

Back in the car she looked at Will, his face a familiar expression of barely reigned-in patience.

"Are you ready?" he asked.

Her heart clunked against her ribs just at the look of him. "Not even close."

But as the engine growled to life, Sadie felt lighter. Like an untethered helium balloon. Even though, as they took off into the night, leaving Vallemont behind, she knew not when, or if, she might ever return.

CHAPTER EIGHT

DARKNESS HAD LANDED by the time their private plane—organised with stunning speed by Will's apparently unflappable assistant, Natalie—hit English soil. While the snow falling through the crisp Vallemontian air had felt dreamy and romantic, London's weather was damp and grey.

A driver was waiting for them at a designated point. "Where to, sir?"

Will gave an address in Borough Market and it wasn't long before they were pulling down a dark concrete alley to a warehouse conversion with rows of arched leadlight windows and striped metal security bars.

Sadie walked hesitantly inside.

Will dragged his battered silver case with Maia the telescope inside to a spot beside a long, black leather couch, then moved about, turning on lights, turning on the heat.

Industrial lamps splashed pools of cool light against walls of rustic exposed brick. Insanely high ceilings criss-crossed with massive steel and wooden beams. There was a fantastical Art Deco staircase that went up, up, up. Huge, gunmetal-grey barn doors shut off whatever rooms were behind them. Everything was dark, seriously arty and hyper-masculine. There was an old wooden plane propeller mounted to the wall above the TV, for Pete's sake!

It was an amazing place, to be sure. Only it didn't mesh with what she thought she knew of Will. Not even close. She would have said Will's defining feature was how confident he was in his own skin—in his cleverness, his quirks, his self-containment. This place was pure mid-life crisis—all it was missing was wood chips on the floor, a Lamborghini in the lounge room and the scent of beer in the air.

Coming here had been a mistake. A huge, colossal mistake.

Will touched her on the shoulder and she near leapt out of her skin.

When she realised he was taking her overnight bag she let out a shaky laugh. "Sorry. I was half expecting the bogeyman to have followed us here."

"We weren't followed. I'm sure."

"Prospero was sure and he's a professional."

"Prospero's neck is so thick he can't turn his head to check his side mirrors."

Sadie laughed and a small measure of her nerves faded away.

Then she realised Will's fingers were still hooked into her bag, on her shoulder, the heat of them tingling through her arm. She let him slide the strap away.

Then she moved further into the space. So much space. "How long have you lived here?"

"I've owned it about eight years. Ten maybe. Quite a place, isn't it?"

"Quite."

"But?"

"Did you hear the but?"

"It's written all over your face."

His arms were crossed as he watched her move through his home, but his face was gentle. He didn't seem to mind her hesitance, he was more... curious than anything else. The Will she knew was curious. Painfully so. It made her nerves fade a little more.

"But...where's all your stuff?"

He looked around. "In its place."

What place? There was nothing there. No rugs

to soften it, no cushions to add comfort. No book-shelves, even though Will was an educated man. No knick-knacks, no family photos. Not even a telescope pointing out the expanse of windows. No sense of Will at all.

"I wasn't expecting company."

She dragged her eyes away from the man cave to shoot Will a flat stare. "Big shock. But even if you were, all of this feels more like a concerted effort to scare people away."

He didn't react. Didn't even blink. But then a smile kicked at the corner of his mouth and his dimple came out to play. Sadie tried to settle the resultant shimmer in her belly, as she wondered if maybe she had him figured out after all.

The she turned on her toes and came to a halt, her mouth dropping open at the huge, twenty-foot-high wall covered in the most stunning wall-paper—a black background scattered with the names of constellations and such in chunky white font.

"That was the clincher," he said, his voice near as he moved in behind her. "My publisher had rented the place and a stylist had decked out that wall for a publicity shoot before my first book came out. I found I wasn't comfortable pretend-

ing the place was mine for the book jacket pho-
tographs, so I bought it. As is. *Stuff*—or lack
thereof—and all."

Sadie wasn't au fait with London real estate
but she knew enough. "Who knew gazing at the
stars paid so well?"

"It's not all star-gazing, Sadie," he said, his
voice going gruff in that way it did when she
had him on the ropes. He was so easy that way.

"No?"

"Consultancy, publishing, speaking, teaching.
I do okay. Not as well as a prince, mind you."

"Ha! Turns out, for me, that's not all that much
of a selling point."

Will's brow clutched. And Sadie, belatedly,
heard what she'd said.

"Not that you were *trying* to sell me anything,
of course." *Stop. Stop talking right now. Nope,
more words coming.* "But if you were... I'm out
of a job, out of a home and on the shelf. You in
the market for a wife?"

It had been a joke. *Absolutely.* She had meant
to alleviate the tension that had been humming
between them since they'd taken off in Will's car.
Or maybe it had been since the first night on the
balcony. Or the first time she'd seen Will's smile.

It didn't work. Tension rippled through the air like a living thing, smacking against the stark brick and overwhelming glass and rocketing back at them like flying knives.

Feeling the pink beginning to rise up her throat, Sadie flapped a lazy hand at Will. "I changed my mind. Now I've seen this place I realise the neat freak thing wasn't a one-off. And I'm a delightful slob. It would never work."

She feigned a nonchalant yawn which turned into the real thing.

"You look exhausted."

"Why, thank you," she said on yet another yawn.

"You hungry?"

"Not a bit," she lied. Knowing she had to head somewhere quiet, alone, to collect her thoughts before she said something even less appropriate than mock-proposing to the guy.

"Then I'll show you to your room."

Sliding the strap of her bag over his shoulder, Will headed for the stairs, leaving Sadie to follow. The heating system must have been state of the art as she was starting to feel all thawed and fuzzy already.

Up the big black stairs they went, past more

barn doors—she spied a sliver of sterile-looking office behind one, fancy gym equipment behind another, which explained the man's physique—until Will stopped in front of a neat, light room with huge, curtainless windows and a view of a whole lot of rooftops of post-industrial London.

Will handed over her bag and waited on the threshold as she went inside. "There's a private bathroom through that door. The remote on the bedside table darkens the windows." A beat. Time enough for his cheeks to lift before he said, "Knowing how much you like borrowed clothes, there are spares in the cupboard."

She sat on the corner of the neat grey bed and patted her bag, holding it close to her chest to try to stop the *ba-da-boom* of her heart at the sight of that smile. "I'm all good."

"Excellent. If I'm not here in the morning there'll be food in the fridge. I'll leave my assistant's contact details on the kitchen bench. She knows where I am at all times."

"Okay."

"Okay. Goodnight, Sadie."

"Goodnight, Will."

Will went to slide the door closed, but Sadie

stopped him with a breath. "They'll figure out who you are, you know."

"I know."

"They'll make assumptions without fact and write about it. They'll take those pictures and turn them into something ugly. Over and over again, the stories getting bigger, wilder, further and further from anything resembling truth." She knew. She'd seen it happen to other members of Hugo's family. Tall poppies ripe for cutting down.

"I'm aware."

"Are you? Because the thought of it impacting your career, of you having to explain me to your friends… I sense that, for all the speaking and publishing and teaching and consulting and international jet-setting, you're a private man, Will. Should you call your family?"

"No family to call."

"None?"

"Sadie, don't worry about it."

"But I will. I do. I worry all the time. The thought of someone out there not liking me, or being angry at me, or blaming me…" She ran a hand over her eyes. "You're right. I am exhausted."

Will's toe nudged over the line at her door before he stopped himself. "Whatever happens to-morrow, or next week, the sun will rise, the earth will turn, and it will be forgotten. We all will be forgotten. Nothing lasts for ever."

Sadie laughed. "Was that meant to make me feel better?"

"You're laughing."

"So I am."

"Sleep."

"Yes, sir."

With that Will slid the door closed, leaving Sadie in his big grey room, in the big, bold house, in a big, strange city, her thoughts a flurry, her heart confused, her oldest fears playing on the edges of her mind.

Alone.

"I'm back."

"The Boss Man's back!" Natalie paused as she mulled over Will's words. "Back to work or back in London? Or back in Vallemont? I've lost track."

Will lay back on his uncomfortable couch in the main room, staring up at the propeller jutting out from the floating wall, wondering if there might be a button somewhere to make it work, he'd simply never cared enough to find out. "London. Work."

"Fantastic! I'll set up newyorker.com for you for…tomorrow afternoon your time. No appointment set up with the prime minister as yet, but I've managed to become firm friends with his secretary, Jenny. She gave me an amazing recipe for mulberry jam. And I can let Garry know he no longer has to berate you for never taking a break, as you've just had two whole days in the gorgeous countryside of Vallemont! Was it amazing?"

"Amazing," Will said.

"You're not even listening."

Will sat up straight. Focused. He checked his watch to find it had been five minutes since the last time he'd looked. And twenty-five minutes since he'd left Sadie to sleep in his spare bedroom.

He rubbed a hand over his chin to find his beard now long enough to leave a rash, and said, "New Yorker. Jam. Sadie. I got it."

"Will."

"Yes, Natalie."

"Who's Sadie?"

Will held the phone away from his ear as if it

had just grown legs. Dammit. How distracted was he.

"Will? Will!" Natalie's voice chirped through the phone.

Will slowly brought it back to his ear. In time to hear his assistant ask, "Is that what you were doing the past two days? A girl?"

Will pinched the bridge of his nose. For all her voracious work ethic and killer travel-arranging skills, Natalie was ridiculously focused on his private life. She had been since she saw a photo of him once in *GQ*, attending the Kennedy Centre honours for a previous president with a Victoria's Secret model on his arm.

The fact that his date was a space buff who'd been in contact with Garry, his manager, asking for advice on which university was best for post-grad studies was beside the point as far as Natalie was concerned.

"Will," she shouted. "Don't you lie to me. It's the one non-negotiable of our contract together."

"No, it's not."

"Fine. But tell me anyway. I worry about you. From all the way over here. Garry does too. And Cynthia."

His publisher? Please don't say they'd all been talking about him.

"Knowing you had a nice girl in your life would go a long way to alleviating our concerns."

"Natalie, do I not pay you enough?"

"Oh, no, Boss Man. I cannot complain on that score. Not a single bit."

"Do I push my luck, ask too much of you, underappreciate you?"

"Often, sometimes and absolutely no."

Not the answer he'd expected. Into the moment's pause Natalie said, "Will, did you or did you not meet a girl in Vallemont?"

He stared up at the propeller once more and thought of the look of incredulity in Sadie's eyes as she'd spotted it. He'd had dates in his London pad before. They'd either not noticed the thing, or they'd thought it inspired. Sadie had known, in a second, that it wasn't something he'd ever have chosen.

"It's complicated."

Natalie whooped. And clapped. For so long he wondered if she was giving him a standing ovation.

"It's not what you think."

"You have no idea what I think."

"You think I'm skiving off work because I've found myself a woman who's made me realise human relationships are more important than work can ever be."

A long pause. "Well, have you?"

"No, Natalie. I have not. For which you ought to be thankful, as it is my work that keeps you in mulberry jam."

Natalie went quiet. Then, "Will Darcy, it is my skill that keeps me in mulberry jam. It's your work that keeps you from rocking in a corner. Check your calendar; it's updated. And packed to the rafters, just as you like it. Goodnight."

Will threw his phone to the end of the couch, where it bounced and settled. Knowing he ought to check his calendar in order to be prepared for the next day's work, he instead headed upstairs, ignoring the lift of his pulse as he passed Sadie's closed door, and headed into his room.

He showered—and shaved, *hallelujah*—put on fresh pyjamas, and hopped into his own bed.

Then stared at the ceiling knowing he'd never been further from sleep in his entire life.

Natalie's words floated around and around his mind like so much space junk.

He had relationships. They were simply shorter,

more condensed or more peripheral than others might be used to.

And, while his work was at the centre of his life, it wasn't the thing that held him together. If he had to give it up one day, he could. Yup, even he heard it—he sounded like a junkie. *Who's Sadie?* Natalie had asked.

Sadie was the reason he felt a gnawing self-reproach at having missed work for two days apart from a little gazing at the Orionid Shower.

Sadie was the reason he was holed up in his London house, when he should be in the outback, a desert, anywhere but the high-density cityscape that was London, where it was so grey out he'd see nothing but soup.

Sadie was the reason he was wide awake.

He rolled over, and closed his eyes. Sleep would come. This restlessness wouldn't last.

Nothing ever did.

Sadie was used to things going bump in the night. She'd grown up in a several-hundred-year-old palace after all.

But it didn't make a lick of difference. As tired as she was, knowing Will was out there was making her restless.

Restless in a way she hadn't been before the kiss on the cheek.

Before the photos of them looking so…so…

Before he'd gone above and beyond, whisking her away to his private residence.

She rolled over, rifled through her overnight bag. Hello! Her phone.

It was only slightly charged. And she had so many messages her mailbox was full. She paused a half-second before deleting it all. And she made the only call she needed to make.

"This is Genevieve."

Sadie rolled her eyes. "It's *me*, Maman. And I know you know because my number comes up when I call."

A beat slid by in which Sadie imagined her mother's imperious stare. Only then did her mother launch into a series of very important questions.

"Mercedes Gray Leonine, did I not teach you anything about getting into cars with strange men?"

"No. You did not."

"Really?"

"It never came up."

A beat, then, "Are his eyes as blue as they look in the photo?"

"Oh, yeah."

"Some might call that extenuating circumstances."

Some, but not Genevieve. It had been her life's mission to make sure her daughter thought once, twice, three times before taking anyone at face value. Men in particular. The better looking, the more charming, the more she was encouraged to stay away. It was as if she'd had to defy her mother by falling for her acting coach in New York—an older man, beautiful but fallible—to finally see she had a point.

Leading her to Hugo. The one man in her life, and her mother's life, who had always been the exception to the rule.

Still Sadie had run. And where had she learned that, again?

"Now Hugo tells me you are *living with* this man?"

"Not living. Staying. In his spare room. He is a dear old friend of Hugo's. He's been amazingly… unruffled by the situation. A self-contained sort of man." Yikes, she was making him sound like a doddering uncle. She heard Will's voice accusing her of *protesting too much* and eased back. "It's easier this way."

"Hmmm. And how good-looking is he?" her mother asked. "Because if that photograph was even close you need to beware—"

"Maman. Any chance we can talk about something other than Will?"

"But why?"

"Because I ran away from marrying a prince yesterday and I thought you might have an opinion on that. And I hear that you have retired and moved out of the palace and I wondered if you would like to hear my opinion on that?"

"Not so much."

Sadie rolled onto her back and stuck her legs in the air, the huge, lacy white nightie she had never seen before that her mother had so kindly packed for her falling to her hips as she twirled her ankles one way and then the other. "I've been thinking."

"Yes?"

"About my father."

Never a fun topic.

Sadie's toes clenched as she waited for her mother's, "I see."

"About the similarities between us."

"You do have his eyes." Genevieve sighed. The love of melodramatics also an inherited trait.

"I mean, that he was a runner. And so, it seems, am I."

"Oh, darling. My sweet girl. What you are is discriminating. You will not be shaken. You will not be swayed. You know kindness and you know how to put people at ease."

"I know when I'm being hustled."

"That's my girl. No point being sweet unless it's wrapped around a core of steel."

"That's right, Maman." Sadie let her feet drop. She rolled to her side, watched moonlight play over the painted wood floor. "Have you really moved out already?"

"I really have. To a lovely little cottage on the edge of the grounds. Marguerite has been saving it for me for years. You have a room here too, my darling. If you want it."

Sadie rolled onto her front, to the foggy grey view out the window, to the light from the converted homes nearby, the city beyond. Growing up in the country, she'd dreamed of living in a big city one day—close to the best theatres, surrounded by crowds and people who had no clue who she was. Who didn't watch her every move. Where she could be anonymous.

New York hadn't worked out. Maybe this was a second chance.

"Thanks, Maman. I'll let you know as soon as I know what I decide to do."

Her phone started to buzz. Low battery. She promised to call soon and hung up.

She rolled to sitting. Her toes reached to the floor before curling away from the cold grey. Only... Her toes tapped against the floor to find it warm. Toasty, in fact. Underfloor heating. Naturally.

She was thirsty. Or hungry. Or something.

Whatever she was she couldn't sit here pretending to sleep. It was early—maybe that was it. She needed to stretch her legs. Or watch a little TV. Hugo had mentioned a book in her bag... No. A book wouldn't do it. Surely this place had a TV somewhere.

Grabbing the heavy comforter off the end of the bed, she wrapped it around her shoulders and heaved open the door and—

The comforter slid off her shoulders and landed in a puddle on the floor as she came face to face with Will.

He'd stopped in the hallway, a cup of coffee in his hand. A pristine white T-shirt—creased from where it had just come out of its packet— did magical things to his chest. Or was that the other way around? Dark grey pyjama bottoms hung low on his hips. His feet were bare.

Moonlight sliced across his strong face. He'd shaved, making him look younger somehow. Clean-cut. All crisp edges, and smooth lines. Much like the statue he seemed too fond of incarnating. Except for the banked heat in his eyes.

"I don't remember that being in my spare-clothes drawer."

"Hmm?" Sadie followed his gaze, glancing down at her matronly nightgown with its neck-to-ankle pin-tucks. "My mother packed it for me."

"Is there a chance she wants you living at home with her for ever?"

Sadie laughed out loud, recalling the phone call she'd literally just had. "Could be."

For a man who came across as so dry, he had a way at cutting to the heart of things. The humanity. Like this strange house of his—cool and intimidating on the outside, but warm to the touch.

"Did you need something?" he asked. His deep voice rumbled over her skin like a blast of heat.

Did she? Did she need something? Maybe. Maybe what she needed was right here in front of her.

No. Don't be stupid. You don't need Will. You've just gotten used to having him near. You like having him near. You want to have him nearer still.

Boy, was that a bad idea. He was Hugo's friend, for one. He was a self-confessed workaholic, existing in the rarefied air of the intelligentsia, whereas everything she did was navigated by her heart. And security was crucial to her; knowing she had a safe place to go home to if everything else in her life fell apart. His home clearly meant nothing more to him than a place to occasionally sleep.

If she stood a chance of doing this right one day, she'd need a stayer. Someone solid and settled and present. Someone to pin her feet to the floor. Someone she could trust not to bolt. Someone not like her father. *Someone not like her.*

She needed someone else.

But she wanted him.

He took a step closer and she gripped the comforter for all she was worth.

"Are you hungry? We could go out— No. Bad idea."

Will smiled. It did things to his face, encouraging things, that had Sadie feeling warm all over. It had to be some kind of glitch in the space-time continuum to find the only astronomer in the universe who could do more for a white T-shirt than Marlon Brando.

"I could order food in. I think Natalie had my cleaning agency pin some takeaway menus to a door somewhere."

She shook her head no.

"How about a book? I know there are plays in my library. Funny, I hadn't remembered until that moment that Clair used to read herself to sleep when it wouldn't come on its own."

Funny; she wondered if he realised that here, alone with her, he was able to say Clair's name and not look as if he was being stabbed in the heart as he said it.

Funny how well he knew her that he understood she was a lover of words.

Not so funny that all of that burned him a little place marker onto her heart.

"The building came with a fully stocked library when I bought it. I'm sure even Shakespeare is in there somewhere."

Maybe it was the moonlight, maybe it was the

man—heck, maybe it was the fact that he kept quoting Shakespeare—but Sadie dropped the comforter on the floor, stepped over it, took Will by the front of the T-shirt, pulled herself up onto her toes and kissed him.

Time seemed to stand still as her lips met his. Her fingers curled harder into the cotton as every nerve ending zinged as if all the energy in all the world had coalesced into her body in that moment.

Which was why it took a moment to realise he wasn't kissing her back.

Her eyes fluttered open to find his dark. Impenetrable.

She pulled back. A fraction. A mile. It didn't matter. So long as she had those eyes on hers. For she knew she hadn't misread the signs—the way he looked at her, how he found excuses to touch her—had she?

The urge to let go, to step back, to apologise, make a joke, make light, to *run* was near overwhelming.

But this time the want was stronger.

She squeezed the cotton tighter in her grip, holding on for dear life. And…there. The thump of his heart against her knuckles gave him away. It was galloping, out of control.

"Will?" she said, her voice barely a breath.

With a growl that seemed to come from some primal place inside of him, Will's arms were around her, holding her so close not a sliver of light could get through, then kissed her like there was no tomorrow.

Colour exploded behind her eyes as heat and want and desire and relief swirled together in a heady mix of intense sensation. His kisses were like a dream, pulling her under until her thoughts were no longer her own.

Her hands ran over his hard shoulders, diving into his curls. Her knees lost all feeling and she felt an almost insatiable need to cry.

Then, just when she thought she might dissolve into a puddle of trembling lust, his arm slid under her knees and she whooped as her feet left the ground.

Laughter spilled from her as Will stepped over the comforter and carried her to the bed. He dropped her so she bounced. Her laughter grew patchy, breathless, as he hovered at the end of her bed.

He stood perfectly still in a patch of moonlight,

every inch of him illuminated in its silvery spotlight.

She felt as though she could see past the impermeable Will wall and into the heart of him for the very first time. Substantial, stoic, strong and sure. But above all solitary. A lone wolf.

Her belly fluttered in warning. *Be careful. Be sure.*

This had all the markers of self-sabotage he'd observed in her. Only it didn't feel the same. It didn't have the same breathless desperation with which she made so many big decisions. She felt... calm. Present. As if she'd been waiting for this moment her entire life.

"What are we doing, Will?"

"If you need me to tell you that—"

"You know what I mean. This, us, it's just a normal reaction to the stress of the past few days, right?"

He said nothing. But she'd been stuck in close quarters with him long enough now to read his supremely subtle body language. The heat was no longer banked, the spark of attraction was aflame. But he was as conflicted as she was.

But then his gaze travelled down her body, roaming over her hair, her shoulders, down her voluminous nightdress to her feet, leopard-print toenails curling and uncurling in the soft grey sheets. It left a trail of warmth, of anticipation, of promise in its wake.

And he said, "I've never been comforted by the idea of normal. Not when there's the option to reach for more."

"All the way to the stars?"

He smiled then, a deeply sexy smile in which his dimple came out to play. Then he climbed onto the bed and thought became something other people did.

His hand started at her ankle, then moved slowly up her calf. She jerked as it hit the back of her knee. Then it was gone, over the top of her nightgown now, sliding over her hip, slowly moving over her ribs. Her muscles melted one by one. All except her toes. They curled so far back on themselves they hurt.

She grabbed him by the T-shirt and dragged him towards her. He caught himself so he didn't hurt her, muscles in his arms straining as he pressed her back, even as she pulled him down.

Then his fingers were at her neck, tracing the edge of her nightgown. She realised he was looking for a button. A release.

She reached down to her knees to grab the hem, before wriggling the acres of fabric over her head. Dangling it daintily over the edge of the bed, she said, "Unless you'd prefer I fold it and place it neatly in my bag…"

Will shoved it to the floor, and hauled her into his arms. The heat of him burnt through his clothes, searing her bare skin. It was as if now he had her he couldn't stand to let her go.

Dangerous thought.

This was a man for whom sentimentality was a four-letter word. He *would* let her go. And that was okay.

Funny; the fact that he would never expect anything from her made him all the more of a prize.

As she hovered on the edge of no turning back, her eyes once more found his, moonlight no longer giving her insight, forcing her to respond to the truth of his touch, his pulse, his presence.

"Nothing's going to be the same, is it?"

He smoothed her hair off her face. Kissed her nose. Her forehead. Her chin. And found her eyes again. "Nothing ever is."

Then he lowered himself to drag his lips across hers, slow, gentle, before settling perfectly into place and stealing her breath away, taking her to some other place where thought was lost, memory became a dream and nothing mattered but the moment.

And neither of them said a thing for a good long while.

CHAPTER NINE

WILL WOKE LATE. Not that he could remember what he might be late for. Or what day it was. Or what country he was in.

Then he heard Sadie shift, muttering and murmuring as she rolled onto her belly, the sheets twisting with her, her hair cascading down her back, like liquid fire in the morning light.

The urge to join her again hit fast and furious. To sweep her hair away and run his hand down her back. To trace her spine with kisses. To see her smile.

To feel her open to him. To silence her moans with a kiss. To see that look in her eyes, the raw emotion, something beyond attraction, beyond a mere spark, as she tumbled over the edge.

But, while the night before had felt inevitable, the burning away of the tension that had simmered between them from the moment he nearly ran her down, waking her with a kiss would be a very different thing.

For he was in London, it was Monday and he had work to do.

Will slid out of Sadie's bed, picked her nightgown up off the floor and shook it out, preparing to fold it. He stopped himself, tossing it on the edge of the bed instead.

Stretching out his limbs, he turned at the door and looked back. Took stock.

He would give her sanctuary so long as she required it, and he could get back to real life, driven by a brutal calendar, living on the rush of his work, banking his meticulously architected reputation to make sure he was in the rooms of power.

But now he had finally slayed the sentimental obstructions that had been dogging him for years, he did not intend to replace one kind with another.

Stepping over the comforter in her doorway, Will went back to work.

Sadie felt like herself for the first time in days. Weeks even.

It could be the jeans.

While packing her a nightgown fit for Queen Victoria, Sadie's all too clever mother had also packed her favourite jeans. Soft from wear, skin-tight and worn away at the knees. Add a warm top, an oversized cream jumper and a leopard-print scarf and she was happy as a clam.

It could also have been the coffee.

She'd managed to find an espresso machine in Will's concrete kitchen and actual ground coffee. Not instant, or pods, but fresh ground: manna from heaven.

Of course, it might well have been Will.

Last night had been...unexpected. Not the fact that it had happened. Something had had to give, what with the tension that had been building be-tween them in incremental steps for days. But the way of him—intense as he was in the everyday, all dark, brooding eyes and devastating detail. But also tender. Cherishing her. Making her ache so sweetly, all over, so deeply, she'd lost all sense of place and time. She didn't remember falling asleep so much as drifting away as if on a cloud.

Then, as though she'd closed her eyes and opened them again, it had been morning. And she'd been fully awake. Every fibre, every cell, every hair follicle switched on. As though the night before had acted like some kind of psychic system reset. As if things would be different from hereon in, she just had to figure out how.

But first...coffee.

Sipping, she stared across the great expanse of Will's plane-hangar-sized abode. The weak morning sunlight did nothing to make the living space appear homelier. While stunning in its über-masculine detail, it was sterile. The perfect pad for the man who'd leapt from his car and accused her of being obtuse.

But what about the man who'd held her in his arms, caressing a length of her hair, breathing softly into her neck as they'd floated into slumber together? There had to be proof of him here somewhere.

She began a room-by-room reconnoitre.

The kitchen cupboards were mostly bare. His office had not a pencil out of place. It was as if he'd deliberately not left his mark on the place. As if being packed, ready to leave a place, wasn't the mark of a well-seasoned traveller but a way of life.

Despite the underfloor heating and the coffee in her system, Sadie suddenly felt the cold.

What brought a man to the point where being alone was the only choice?

The few times Sadie had managed to solicit her mother to talk about her father, Genevieve had admitted she'd been smitten. That his passion, his joie de vivre, his dashing good looks had been hard to resist. That she'd been so blinded by it she'd never for a moment imagined he'd desert her the way he had.

Cradling the cooling coffee, she wandered aimlessly about the upper level, bypassing small doors probably leading to storage areas and a ladder that went up to who knew where.

And then she found the library.

She stepped inside the cool, shadowy room. The heavy dark shelves were covered in books organised by colour and shape rather than author or title. Visually stunning, but futile.

Nevertheless, she searched. For something she couldn't be sure was there but was certain all the same. Going over each row, each column until… There.

She pulled down the textbook, its pages soft and heavy in her hands. Then she turned it over to see the cover, her heart lodging in her throat at the words on the cover—*Waiting to Be Known* by Dr Will Darcy.

Swallowing hard, she looked inside. The title, it

explained, was taken from a quote by Carl Sagan. Reviews included praise by famous scientists. The dedication read simply, *"For Clair."*

She flicked through the rest to find that from there it went into full scientific-textbook mode. Words upon words, diagrams, maths and the occasional colour picture to break it up. Clever man, this friend of Hugo's. This friend of hers.

But waiting to be known? Could it be?

She put the book down and looked a little further until she found a large, softcover book amongst the hardbacks. Its spine was creased with use. A book someone had actually read.

She pulled *The Collected Works of William Shakespeare* from the shelf. Opened it to find dog-ears. A handful of notes in the margins. The sign she'd been looking for. The sign *someone* had lived here. Someone had left something of themselves behind.

A piece of paper fell out. A receipt that had been used as a bookmark. By the date, it had been bought after Will had moved in, meaning Will had bought the book himself. Read it. Made notes.

She brought the heavy tome to her chest, pressing it against her rocketing heart. The brand he'd burned there the night before pulsed like a fresh wound as the tendrils of his life twisted a little tighter around hers.

Why was she doing this to herself? Looking for connections? Just because she felt as if she'd glimpsed the core of the man, it didn't mean she ought to keep digging. It didn't mean that knowing him, understanding him, would get her what she wanted.

And she wanted… No.

Will had said it himself—she had a predilection for self-sabotage. Or maybe, she was beginning to wonder, was it more of a compulsion? Do unto herself before someone else did unto her.

If so, not any more.

She'd woken up that morning and she was never going to fall asleep to her life again.

It was long dark by the time Will returned.

And it had been a hell of a day. Determined to get back on track, he'd made a dozen phone calls, finished research papers and begun others, fitting a trip out to the Royal Observatory with a meeting with the gaming crew. He felt as if he could only remember half of it. Probably for the best, as the game had major holes—meaning he had to front up more money, and agree to replace one of the designers, in order to get it back on track. A paper was rejected, as the core theory had already been covered by a fellow scientist from Tulsa. And Natalie was still stubbornly unhappy with him for not being more "sharing".

Music was playing as he headed to the front door and for a second he found himself checking he was outside the right warehouse. When he opened the door he was overcome with the scent of home cooking.

It was so foreign, so specifically outside the basic absolutes of his life, and yet so sorely welcome after such a long, difficult day, he nearly shut the door.

But then he heard the clang of pots and pans. His natural curiosity had him edging inside to find Sadie behind the kitchen bench wearing an apron he didn't know he had, using pots he'd never seen, dancing along with Otis Redding coming from a record player somewhere, cooking up a storm.

She looked up, lips puckered around the end of a wooden spoon, then slid the spoon away before calling, "Honey, you're home!"

It was so sexy Will found himself in the middle

of an out-of-body experience—pleasure warring with good judgment. He gripped his briefcase hard enough to break.

Then she burst into laughter. "I'm kidding! Oh, my God, you should see your face. Come in. Put down your stuff. Sit. And wipe that look of abject terror off your face. All this is me going a very small way to making it up to you for being my babysitter, and my bodyguard, my newfound friend."

Will found himself holding his breath as he waited for another title. When none came it felt insufficient.

He dropped his briefcase by the couch, then moved towards the kitchen. Antennae on the blitz, he wasn't sure whether to kiss her on the cheek and ask after her day, or keep the bench safely between them.

In the end, he moved around to the working side of the bench. Plates and cutlery, napkins and wine glasses were lined up ready to be filled. He looked in the pot. Some kind of soup was bubbling away. It smelled amazing. Rich, decadent and wholesome.

"Where did you find all this?"

"In the cupboards. And a local grocery store delivered the ingredients."

"You cooked this?"

"Of course I cooked this. I'm fixing things in reverse, you see. Stitching up the mess I've made, starting with thanking you."

He looked up to find her nudged in beside him. Not touching, but close enough to see the light dusting of flour on her cheek. The sparks of gold in the ends of her hair sticking out of the messy topknot on her head. Her jeans fitted like a second skin and on her feet she wore a pair of socks he would have sworn were his.

Tendrils of attraction curled around him like a fast-motion creeper, twisting and tugging, shooting off in random directions until he couldn't tell where it all began. "I assumed…"

"That I lorded it up in the palace? I *learnt* in the palace. Thank goodness too. When I lived in New York I shared a tiny studio apartment with three other starving actors who waited on tables on the side. I worked in hotels, so I didn't get any of the leftover food they did. For me it was cook or starve."

"You lived in New York."

Her gaze swept to his. Snagged. Whatever she

saw in his gaze had her pupils growing dark. A pulse beat in her neck.

Brow furrowing, she moved away from him to clean a bench that already looked pretty clean. "For a few years, in fact. In order to…expand my dramatic education. Why? Do I seem that parochial?"

"Yes."

She laughed, the sound tinkling up into the rafters. And Will found himself imagining coming home to this every day. Not the food, though his taste buds were watering like crazy. The woman. Her smile, her impudence, her interminable optimism.

"I get that," she said. "But, as I keep telling you, you didn't meet me at my best. I can be quite erudite when the situation calls for it. Charming too. And I know some of the best dirty jokes you will hear in your life."

Will breathed out hard, trying to find some kind of equilibrium. He was so out of sync, he felt like coming through his own front door and trying again.

It was his fault. Work or no work, he shouldn't have left as he had, not without discussing what had happened. Without putting their night together into some kind of sensible model—with margins, and objectives, and a deadline.

He'd just have to do it now.

First, he turned to pour himself a large glass of water, but he stopped when he saw the open book on the bench next to the fridge. His textbook. Open to a page about a third of the way through. A couple of bookmarks fashioned out of kitchen towel poked out of the top. And she'd scrawled question marks in the margin.

"You read my book?"

"You read Shakespeare. Seemed a fair exchange. Hungry?" she asked.

"Famished," he said, his voice a growl.

She ladled a hefty amount of soup into each bowl, tore some bread apart and lathered it in butter, then finished the look with a small pinch of herbs. *"Voilà!"*

Will breathed it in. And rubbed a hand up the back of his neck.

"You okay? You look like no one ever cooked you soup before."

"The kitchen at my grandmother's place was three floors down and locked away in the servants' quarters. The house smelled like demoral-isation and thousand-year-old paintings. It never smelt like this."

"Well, then, you're welcome." A second slunk by before she said, "You were raised by your grandmother, weren't you? Were your parents not around?"

"They died when we were five."

"That's rough. I can't imagine not having my own mother around, baffling woman that she is. Is that why you always call it your grandmother's place and not home?"

"As you call the place you grew up 'the palace'."

"Huh. Do I really?"

He looked to Sadie, hip nudged against the bench, holding a glass of wine in her hand, watching him. She was the very picture of friendly nonchalance.

Except he knew better. For all the happy chatter, she was on edge. Her energy level was at altissimo, pitching and keening. His pitched with it. An echo. Her shadow. The dark to her light. North to her south.

He moved in closer.

She swallowed, her wine dropping a fraction.

"Nowhere I've lived has ever smelt like this."

"Because I live out of a suitcase, Sadie."

"Or a soft black bag and battered silver telescope case."

He smiled and it felt good. The best he'd felt all day since leaving her bed. "Or that. The truth is I can't stay in one place longer than about a month before it starts to feel too comfortable, my work suffers and I leave. Relationships follow the exact same pattern. I don't like it when my work suffers. When it suffers—"

"You suffer?"

He moved in closer again and she put the wine on the bench.

"The data I am able to collect, collate, decipher and impart is important."

"To whom?"

"To the entire world."

An eyebrow kicked north. "Wow. That's a lot of pressure."

"I like pressure," said Will, moving in close enough that the tips of his leather shoes prodded her socks. "I live for the pressure. Pressure is my bliss."

Sadie crossed her arms but her feet stayed put. "Will, is this some kind of warning?"

"Sadie, since you came into my life I have no bloody idea what I'm doing."

He slid a hand into Sadie's hair, tucking his hand over the back of her neck. He gave himself a moment to soak in those eyes, the freckles, energy enough to keep this place alight for a week.

"Wait," she said on a whisper, "what are we doing?"

"Again, if you need me to tell you that—"

"Will."

It was the perfect moment to explain to her the margins and objectives, and a deadline.

Instead he ran his thumb over her cheek and leaned towards her. Her mouth opened on a sigh just before he put his lips to hers.

A second later her hands crept up his chest, sliding under his collar and pulling his head closer. She opened to him, pressing her body against his. Making sweet little murmuring sounds as she melted into his arms.

He held her tighter still. So tightly she lifted off the ground. Swinging her around, he sat her on the bench.

Her eyes flashed open and her hands flew away as the cool of the concrete seeped into her jeans. And then she smiled against his lips.

This. This was what he'd been thinking about all day. Coming home to this. The intimacy he'd been avoiding his entire adult life. It was terrifying. It was irresistible.

She pulled back just enough to slide his jacket from his shoulders, letting it drop to the floor.

"You're a bad influence," he murmured as he tried to go in for another kiss.

But she pushed him away, moving to undo the buttons of his shirt, one by slow damn one. Once his shirt joined his jacket she ran a hand over his chest, following the line of the now purple and yellow bruise. "Does it hurt?"

"Not right now."

She laughed, the sound sexy as hell.

Then she kissed the bruise, right at the top, and Will sucked in a breath. He held it still as she pulled him into the cradle of her thighs and kissed him. On the jaw, the cheek, the tip of his nose.

Her kisses were so delicate, so exquisite, he felt as if he could barely hold himself together. As if he might crack right down the middle if he breathed too hard.

But then she touched her lips to his, ran her tongue over the seam and tugged his head to hers and he fell apart anyway.

He'd been overachieving by every quantifiable measure of success. But it had been a straight and narrow road. He hadn't been living until that moment.

Pathways opened up inside of him as he ran his hands over Sadie's hair, as he pressed into her warmth and swallowed her gasp in a kiss that changed his world.

He grabbed her by the backside and lifted her off the cold kitchen bench. She wrapped her arms about his neck and didn't break the kiss for even a breath as he carried her upstairs. But still Will held on tight.

She had a habit of running when the going got tough. Making her feel safe enough to stay would take finesse, timing and patience. The hours he'd spent behind the eyepiece of a telescope attempting to focus on precise celestial bodies light years away proved he had the staying power.

At the top of the stairs he turned left, heading into his room this time.

They never did get around to eating that soup.

"Do you have a warmer coat?"

Sadie looked up from her coffee to find Will had come home early. Then down at the clothes she'd had on the day before. Her underwear was clean, so she figured that was winning. "I do not."

"Wait here."

"Okay."

Will ducked back upstairs, into his bedroom, and came out with a familiar black tracksuit top.

"Hello, old friend!" she said, putting it on under her jumper, letting the hood fall out of the top. "Now what?"

"Now we go out."

"We can't go out."

"Well, we can't stay here. Not for ever."

"If we go out there someone might see you."

"I've been seen before."

"But they'll see *me*, with you."

"Let them."

He gave her a look then, a look she'd never been given in her life before. Yet she understood it all the same. Deep down in the most primal, private, female part of her she knew.

Will Darcy was staking his claim. Not for ever. He didn't believe in for ever. But for now. Which, for him, was still a very big deal.

"Are you sure about this?"

Will took her by the hand and tugged her into

his arms. "I called our friend the Prince this morning."

Whoa. "And said what?"

Will rubbed away the frown that popped up above her nose. "I gave him a brief, G-rated, run-down of your stay. He asked how the soup was. I changed the subject."

She coughed out a laugh.

"We had a long talk about many things and found ourselves in absolute agreement."

"You did?"

They had. "The first thing we agreed on was that the mourning period was over. The photos of us are true and the world has to get over the fact that they are out there. Time to get on with getting on."

"The palace won't like it."

"The palace can bite me."

"Wow, Will Darcy, them's fighting words."

"I was always good in a fight, even as a kid. Scrappy. Not one for following the rules. I've also never been one to skulk in doorways, and I don't plan on making a habit of it now. So what do you say?"

But she couldn't say a single thing. She was too busy trying to find her feet. Not sure whether to laugh or cry or scream, or turn cartwheels. The only thing she didn't have the urge to do was run. She simply placed her hand in the crook of his arm and smiled.

Outside, the day was glorious. Freezing, as if the first tendrils of real winter were coming, but sunny.

Sadie took a great big, bracing breath. "Are we waiting for the car?"

"I thought we'd walk." And off they went.

Once they hit the end of his street, the crowds began to swell. Tourists and locals. Shoppers and workers. A bustling, noisy, energetic mob.

Being around people once more, for the first couple of minutes Sadie panicked any time someone looked their way, but as Will pointed out landmarks—places he drank coffee, a half-court where he played basketball, the Shard—she began to relax. Besides, no one looked at her twice. Not when she had Will at her side. He drew enough gazes, both admiring and envious, for the both of them.

"So, what do you think?" he asked.

Sadie smiled at Will before realising what he was looking at. A good-sized Tudor building—white with brown trim—lay just ahead.

The Globe Theatre—the modern-day "home" of William Shakespeare.

Sadie wasn't sure she could feel any happier than she did in that moment. Until Will pulled two tickets out of his pocket. *"Much Ado About Nothing*—what do you think?"

Speechless, she nodded. And followed as Will led her inside.

And as the play unfolded before her, a simple, brilliant telling of a complex, bittersweet tale, she knew she was done forcing Shakespeare down the throats of high-school kids who weren't even close to being ready to appreciate the language she loved so dearly.

It was a job she had revelled in for its battles and its victories. A job that had fallen her way. A job people expected her to love.

Just as New York had been something everyone had assumed would be a dream come true.

But defying expectations wasn't such a bad thing. And if it meant following her heart, doing what made her happy, and tapping into her bliss, then even if people didn't quite understand the choice, surely that had to be better than the alternative.

She glanced at Will to find him watching her.

And, not caring if anyone was watching, if anyone knew who they were, she gave him a smile that started at the little place marker he'd burned onto her heart. She slipped her hand through his arm, leant her head on his shoulder and let Beatrice and Benedick sweep her off her feet.

Will could not remember the last time he'd taken a morning off work on purpose. But it had been worth it.

He'd followed the play to a point, but had found Sadie far more entertaining: the spark in her eyes, the grin that near split her face in half and the tears when everything came good. She saw the world like someone who was on earth for the very first time.

She was practically skipping as they left the theatre. "That was amazing. Just…wonderful. It's been so long since I've seen a real, live, professional Shakespearean production not put on by sixteen-year-old kids. I feel like I've been banging my head against a wall for years! That, Will Darcy, was an epiphany. I cannot thank you enough." She threw herself at him then, wrapping him in a hug that took him only a second or two to return. "Now I have to check out the gift shop."

While she did so, Will checked his phone. A dozen calls had come in while his phone had been on silent.

Not wasting time to check the messages, he rang Natalie.

"Hello?"

Will checked his watch. Dammit. It was late over there. "Natalie, apologies. I didn't check the time—I'll call back later."

"No, wait! Give me a second to get to my desk." Much shuffling and banging of doors, a squeak of a desk chair and… "Right. So I've been on to his secretary and she seems to think we've lost our chance but—"

"Sorry. Whose secretary?"

"Ah, the prime minister's." A pause, then, "Did you not get my messages?"

"I've yet to listen—"

"Why on earth? You always check your messages. In fact, you're pedantic to the point of anally retentive. My cousin Brianna read somewhere that men with your looks, your brains and your sex appeal—"

"Natalie."

"Yes. Sorry." A breath, then, "He had space for you this afternoon. At two. Then he was flying out of the country for eight days."

Will checked his watch. It was a little after four.

"Send me the number, I'll call—"

"I've already checked. It's too late, Will. He's gone."

Eyelids lowering, Will swore. Swore some more. Then pressed his phone against his forehead.

"Will? Will, are you there?"

"Thanks for trying, Natalie."

"That's okay. I wish I could have done more."

"It's not your fault," he said, right as Sadie came out of the gift shop, her gaze scanning the area before landing on him. "It's mine."

Something was wrong.

After all the excitement of the play, the sweet thrill of freedom and the hot, burning delight of love that was pulsing through her like radio waves, all the extra layers in the world couldn't have saved her from Will's chill.

Once they were back inside the warehouse, thawing out, she got up the guts to ask, "Will, is everything okay?"

"No, actually."

"What happened?"

"It's nothing. A work matter."

As soon as he mentioned work, she felt him pulling away, heading into a bubble inside his head. Her instinct was to let him, but something bigger made her reach out and clamp a hand around his arm.

"Will, tell me. Maybe I can help."

He looked at her then, the creases at the edges of his eyes deeper, but not from smiling. Her heart slowed, her blood turning sluggish, as if preparing itself for a winter freeze.

"I may have mentioned my old professor at some point."

Her memory skipped and raced until it found the moment she was looking for. "The one who encouraged you to wonder."

"He passed away earlier in the year, not long before your wedding invitation arrived, in fact. Which is by the by. Anyway, he had been pointman for a research grant at our old university for decades. On his death it was marked to shut down. It's cumbersome and prohibitively expensive. But it's also imperative to the long-term success of astronomical research in this country."

"What an amazing legacy."

Will's eyes flashed and she thought she had him back, but he ran a hand up the back of his neck, dislodging her hold on his arm at the same time.

"I was guaranteed a chance to meet with the prime minister to urge him to continue the grant and have been waiting for news of the time. It came through this morning while we were walking. The meeting was set for the same time the play began."

Sadie swallowed, the burn of ignominy tingling all over her skin. "Can't you reschedule? Go bang on his door, right now?"

Will looked down at the floor, hands deep in the pockets of his jeans. What had Hugo said? Will wasn't an island unto himself, he was a planet.

"Will—"

"My work, my achievements, my reputation open doors for me where others wouldn't even get a look-in. But this was my chance. My last chance to truly honour a man who made all that possible. I forgot myself and screwed it up."

Sadie's stomach clutched at the disappointment

in his voice. Worse than disappointment. Devastation.

Her throat was like a desert as she said, "It's my fault."

He looked at her then, really at her. And she realised in that moment that he held her heart in his hands.

"It's mine. For thinking I could do this."

Sadie didn't ask what "this" was. She didn't have to. She'd been right with him as this thing between them had played out, unravelling, exploding, taking them over. She'd held his hand on the street, she'd felt his eyes on her as they'd watched the play. They'd both been held in thrall of a moment in time where their worlds had aligned and all things had seemed possible.

He was determined to take the blame, but Sadie knew it was all her. This was what she did. She got intoxicated by possibility, by the chance that this time things would be different. She dragged others along for the ride, only to end up bathing them in her chaos.

She wrapped her arms around herself in an attempt to stop the trembles that were taking her over, years of practice helping her summon a smile from nowhere. "Don't be so hard on yourself. You've been amazing. Heroic even. I know how much you've sacrificed in rescuing this damsel in distress. And if there's anything I can do to make it up to you—"

"You are no damsel, Sadie, and right now I've never felt less heroic in my life."

He gave her a long look. Of ruination and despair. But beneath it all hummed that heat. The magnet that kept pulling them back together even when circumstance, fate and history had tried telling them it wasn't to be.

It felt as if the universe was holding its breath.

Then he took a step away. "You're right. I can't take no for an answer. I need to attempt to fix this. Look, do you mind if I...?"

"Go. Go! I can take care of myself."

"Good. Thank you, Sadie." Then he jogged up the stairs towards his office, pulling the door shut behind him.

And Sadie brought a shaking hand to cover her mouth.

She was in love with Will.

She knew it. She'd spent the morning bathed in it like a divine glow. But even that hadn't been enough to stop her from being his downfall.

Sadie couldn't feel her feet as she made her way

to her room. And there she slowly, deliberately, packed her things.

She took off Will's jacket, folded it neatly and put it onto the chair in her room. She made the bed, tucking in the corners like an expert. She grabbed some tissue and wiped down every surface she'd touched.

All she'd ever wanted was to feel safe somewhere. Or with someone. Even while her life raged in chaos around her, she'd felt safer the past three days in Will's company than she could remember feeling ever before. His stoic strength, his quiet confidence, were like a balm to her frenetic soul.

Which was a big part of why loving Will, and leaving him, meant now she was scared. Terrified. Shaken from the top of her head to the tips of her toenails.

But she had to do this. For him.

With one last look around the room she made her way to Will's office.

He was on the phone, pacing, papers strewn across the surface of his desk.

He was an important man doing important work. Work that he believed made him the man he was. Sadie would have begged to differ, but she knew he wouldn't hear it right now even if she stripped naked, sat on him and forced him to listen.

He put his hand over the microphone. "Sadie, sorry, you're going to have to give me some time here."

"I'm going one better." She hitched her bag on her shoulder and he stopped pacing.

Grey clouds swarmed over his face. He opened his mouth, no doubt to tell her she was being dramatic, and maybe she was, but she stopped him with the international sign for stop. "I've called a car service. They'll be here in ten."

Running a hand down his face, he hung up the phone and strode around the desk until they were toe to toe. The creases around his eyes were so deep, so concerned. Frustration poured off him in waves. "Do you really have to do this now?"

"I really do. It's past time. And you know it too."

Hands on hips, he looked over her shoulder, into the middle distance, his big brain working overtime. "I'm not a selfless man, Sadie. I'm not going to make a song and dance out of this. I'm not Hugo."

"I'm very glad you're not Hugo." It ached not to

tell him why. To tell him that she loved his particular brand of strength. His stoicism. She loved his stubbornness and his lonesomeness.

She loved him.

"You've been incredible, Will. A good friend to Hugo. A good friend to me. You gave me sanctuary when I needed it most. But you've given up enough to help us. Too much. Today proved that."

She tried to put it into words he'd understand. *Nothing lasts for ever.* But the words wouldn't come. It hurt too much.

Instead she leaned in, placed a hand on the bruise over his heart and kissed him on the cheek. Then, because she wasn't perfect, she took him by the chin, fresh stubble scraping the pads of her fingers, and turned his face so she could kiss his beautiful lips.

He resisted, caught in that vortex of disappointment and frustration. But only for a fraction of a second. Then he hauled her against him and kissed her with everything he had.

If it had been any other man kissing her so that her kneecaps melted, she might have put it down to the urge to get his own way. But Will was not a game player. He was a man of integrity and might.

If she was a betting girl she might have thought that kiss was his way of showing her he was beginning to fall for her too.

But all bets were off. It was time for her to go.

She pulled away, pressed herself back, held herself together by the barest thread. "Thanks, Will. For everything."

He said nothing. No goodbyes. No understanding nods.

But neither did he look like a statue. He looked ravaged, like a man braced against a perfect storm.

Holding that image in her heart, she turned and walked away, down the stairs, out the front door and into the car waiting to take her to the airport. Where she'd take her chances with being recognised, holding her head high.

For she was running again, but this time it wasn't out of fear. This time she was running away for love.

As the tears ran down her face she felt as if she'd done the absolute right thing for the first time in her life.

No one would throw her a parade, or pat her on the head and tell her *well done*. She'd make no new fans out of this. But she knew, and that was what mattered.

CHAPTER TEN

SADIE PARKED HER car under a tree, leapt over the ancient, crumbling brick wall edging the field and walked across the same expanse over which she'd fled not that long ago.

The bottoms of her jeans were soon damp, her boots beginning to chill. But she ploughed on until she found herself standing outside the antechamber, staring up at the façade of the palace.

It was strange to think she had grown up here, and now it only looked like a building. A beautiful building, to be sure, glorious and charming and strong. But it was no longer her home.

Not about to head up to the front door and knock, but also not keen on bumping into anyone in the private quarters, she went with a hunch, pushed her way through the garden brambles and tested the window. It opened easy as pie.

It was ironic to find herself climbing in through the very same window out of which she'd climbed just a few days ago. Or maybe it was necessary. A kind of bookend.

The antechamber was much as she'd left it bar the wedding paraphernalia, which was no doubt at the bottom of a rubbish bin somewhere.

She checked through the door to make sure the coast was clear, then headed off, through the palace.

Five minutes and a few close calls later, Sadie sat huddled beneath the fluffy, double-thick blanket she'd nicked from the back of a couch in the library, secure in her favourite spot in the palace. She was atop the turret of the tallest tower, feet dangling over the side, the country she loved at her feet.

Her gaze tripped over snow-capped mountains, verdant green fields dotted with fluffy black and white sheep. Over the lights of a dozen quaint villages tucked into valleys and sprawled over hillsides.

One of them had to be the village of Bellponte in which she and Will had stayed. If she'd seen the palace from La Tulipe, then surely she could see La Tulipe from here. But she'd never had much of a sense of direction, and couldn't be sure.

Shivering, Sadie tucked her feet up beneath her and wrapped the blanket tighter.

She hadn't realised it at the time, but her life had changed in that chintz-filled tower room. She'd grown up, faced her demons, faced herself. And she'd begun to fall in love.

"Hey."

Sadie sniffed, wiped her cheek against her shoulder and spun to find Hugo framed by the heavy brick doorway.

He said, "Only the Keeper of the Flags is meant to have a key to this spot."

Sadie lifted a finger from its warm cocoon to tap the side of her nose. "I have contacts."

Hugo ambled to Sadie's side. He sat, then swore at the freezing cold of the brick beneath his hands.

Sadie offered him some of her blanket. He refused with a manly shake of the head.

Together, in silence, they looked out over Vallemont as they had a zillion times before. He'd first brought her up here when she was six or seven. She'd also found him here a few weeks back, after Prince Reynaldo had made him the offer he couldn't refuse.

Sadie asked, "How did you know I was here?"

"At least half a dozen people told me they'd seen you sneaking through the palace, heading this way."

"Oh. I thought I'd made it without being seen."

"A running theme in your life of late."

Sadie groaned. "Tell me about it. A few hours ago I thought I'd made it all the way through Heathrow unseen before a pair of Americans asked me for a selfie."

Hugo shot her a smile. "And there I was thinking you were still in London. In fact, I had the funny feeling you were going to be there for some time."

"Nah. This is where I belong." Sadie rested her chin against her knees and glanced at her old friend. "If I hadn't run, would you have gone through with it?"

"Of course," said Hugo without missing a beat.

"Even though you don't love me, and never have."

"I do—"

"Hugo, come on. Does your tummy tighten every time you lay eyes on me? Do you come out in goosebumps if I simply brush your arm? Do you ache for me when we're apart?"

Hugo's silence was answer enough.

"Then consider yourself lucky one of us was smart enough to walk away."

Hugo nodded. "Done." And like that they put the Great Hiccup of their lifelong friendship behind them.

Then, with a bump to her shoulder with his, Hugo asked, "When did you develop such specific parameters for what it means to be in love?"

Sadie bit her lip.

"Because I've never heard you talk that way. You're always so blasé about such things. I'm assuming this is a new development. Very recent, in fact. Days old, at the very most."

"Drop it."

"No, I don't think I will. Why aren't you in London, Sadie?"

If she could have pulled the blanket over her head she would have. But that would have been the old Sadie—make a joke of things, do a little tap dance to distract everyone from anything unpleasant.

So why wasn't she in London? As difficult or ugly as they might be, the new Sadie was all about the truths.

The truth was she might not physically be there, but her heart was. And her head. And she wasn't going to sit there and do nothing about that any more.

She pulled herself to standing and threw Hugo the blanket.

"Come on, get up."

"Why?"

"You and I have some work to do."

A week later Will sat staring at his laptop.

Or *through* his laptop would have been a more fitting description, as the words of the position paper he was attempting to outline were swimming before his eyes.

He could be doing this on a plane to Geneva, where he was due to present his famous "Scenes from the Orion Nebula" lecture the next day. He did some of his best work on planes, alone, uninterrupted, the white noise creating a prefect creative cocoon.

Instead here he sat, in a village pub, with no Wi-Fi and limited phone reception, waiting to feel the satisfied glow that came from one of the best weeks of his career.

An offer had come through on the Orion Nebula game, and he'd sold, tripling his investment overnight.

An array of radio telescopes in Chile had picked up space noise for a few seconds in the direction of Orion's Belt and he'd been there to hear it.

He'd been offered the European Space Agency's top spot on the Future Commission—focusing on how best to channel research and funding for telescopes to be launched into space.

Best of all, an unknown benefactor had gifted five years to the Templeton Grant. Natalie had connected the call from the prime minister, who'd bashfully agreed to join forces now that he didn't have to justify the initial expense, promising to announce it at the World Science Symposium later that year.

But no glow came.

His phone rang. In pure relief, he answered it without looking at the caller details. "Darcy."

"Where are you?"

Hugo. Will sat up so fast he knocked his beer, the froth sloshing over the rim and onto his laptop.

Mopping it up with a napkin, he said, "Is everything all right? Is she okay?"

Hugo laughed. "Sadie's fine. As far as I know."

"What do you mean, as far as you know? Isn't she with you?"

"Of course she's not with me, you damn fool. In fact— No. Yes. I'm going to say it. She should be with you."

Wincing, Will screwed the napkin into a ball. "You don't know what you're talking about."

"I'm a well-educated man. I have seen the world. And I am a prince. Therefore, I am never wrong."

It was so unlike Hugo to pull the prince card, Will actually coughed out a laugh.

"She left of her own free will," said Will.

"Did you ask her to stay?"

"You know as well as I do that there's no telling her anything. I've never met anyone as stubborn." *As quick to laughter, as emotional, bright, indefatigable, raw, sweet, thoughtful, warm.*

"Hmm. I feel as if I have."

Will tossed the damp napkin onto the table.

Hugo went on. "I have never seen you as relaxed as you were when you were with her. She was the best thing that ever happened to you, my friend. How the hell could you have let her go?"

Will knew Hugo was pushing for a reaction. He was good at it.

"Right back at you," Will gritted out, unsurprised when Hugo laughed down the phone.

"So, where are you?"

Will looked up from his laptop at the rustic walls, the craggy-mountain motif carved into the bar, the framed picture of the reigning Prince of Vallemont on the wall, the pink and rose-gold trim on the bar towels. All he said was, "In a pub."

"Alone?"

Alone. Funny how that word had been his touchstone for so many years. A motivator, a goal. He'd held on to the fact that his aloneness gave him an edge, time and motivation to work hard, to better focus, to give himself over to the study of the whys of the universe.

Now the word felt like an open wound.

"Yes, I'm alone. I just felt the need to stretch my legs."

Stretching them all the way to a small pub in Vallemont. With a view over the thatched roof-tops of Bellponte to the top corner of a crumbling hotel with a lopsided Tower Room that looked as though it might fall off the side of the building at any moment.

Will asked, "I am an important man with much work to do. Did you call me for a reason?"

"Go online, stream Vallemontian station, Channel Four, at five o'clock our time."

"And why would I want to do that?"

"Because, old friend, for all the stars and moons and planets and galaxies you have unravelled in your search for the meaning of life, I'd bet the palace it won't compare to what Channel Four is about to teach you."

Will drummed his fingers against the table top and looked up at the TV playing silently above the bar. The logo at the bottom of the screen said Channel Four. If that wasn't a sign he had no idea what was. "Fine. I'll track it down."

"My work here is done," said Hugo, and then he was gone.

Will checked his watch. Fifteen minutes until five.

He closed his laptop and worked on his beer. A low hum of pub chatter and occasional laughter punctuated clinking glassware and the ting of the cash register as Will watched the clock tick down.

Just on five a "special presentation" graphic flashed onto the screen.

A young woman's smiling face mouthed words Will couldn't hear. Closed-caption text scrolled across the bottom of the screen, stating the journalist's name, stipulating that she was a former pupil of the Vallemont School of Drama and therefore a one-time student of Mercedes Gray Leonine, and was happy to be able to facilitate the evening's special event.

And then…there she was.

Will felt his stomach drop away at the sight of her. Her mussed red hair was slicked back and pinned off her face with a clip. Long, sparkly earrings swung against her shoulders and a pale floral top clung to her elegant frame.

She looked different—still, somehow, serene. She looked so beautiful it hurt to blink. And even with the sound turned down he could hear her voice. The bravado. The humour. The strength. The vulnerability. As if she were sitting right beside him.

God, how he wished she were sitting beside him. How he wished he could touch her, hold her, kiss her, hear her voice for real; watch her animated face as she told a story; watch her quiet face as she listened to one of his.

For a man who didn't believe in wishes, they came so thick and fast he couldn't keep up.

The interviewer leaned forward and the camera pulled out to show Sadie sitting on a white couch in a large, old-fashioned-looking room that was no doubt in the palace. And there Hugo sat, right beside her.

Even without sound it was clear how fond they were of one another. Nothing more. No romantic tension. No sideways glances. Just friendship. And honest remorse at the way things had been handled.

"Turn it up!" someone called from across the room. "The TV—turn it up."

The barkeeper did as asked, and Sadie's voice blasted across the pub.

"Our reasons were private, but we hope you believe us when we say they were just and good. We were blinded by a need to do the right thing; we just…didn't think things through to their logical conclusions. And if a man like Prince Alessandro says he'll marry you it's pretty hard to say no. Just look at him!"

The interviewer laughed. Blushed. A woman at a table behind Will said, "Oh, I'm looking."

"If you take anything from this interview, know that your Prince is one of the very best men you could ever hope to meet. Second-best at worst. He's just not the man for me."

And then Sadie looked into the camera. She looked right into Will's eyes. It was a split second, a blink. But he felt that look as if she'd reached out and grabbed him by the heart and squeezed.

"And you, Prince Alessandro—is Mercedes not the woman for you?"

He smiled, and Sadie turned to him, which was when Will saw the clip in her hair. Silver, sparkly, a shooting star.

Will didn't realise he was on his feet until someone behind him politely asked him to sit down.

"Don't answer that," she said. "He'll just say something charming so as not to hurt my feelings. But I'd have driven the Prince crazy. And Vallemont does not need a crazy prince. Look at Prince Reynaldo—such a benevolent leader, so forward-thinking. So generous."

Will noted that Hugo looked down at that point, hiding a wry smile.

"Not only on a personal level—having always been so kind to me, the daughter of a palace maid. Did you know he's recently personally invested in a number of international grants towards the arts and sciences, making Vallemont not only the most beautiful country in the world, but also one of the most progressive?"

The interviewer looked dutifully amazed. "Well, that is news."

The interviewer then turned to Hugo, asking him a spate of questions that Will barely heard. While Sadie leant back in the chair and breathed out long and slow. Only then did Will see how tired she seemed, the slight smudges under her eyes that even television make-up couldn't quite hide.

Sitting through the rest of the interview was the hardest thing Will had ever done in his entire life, but he had to, in case she had any more hidden messages for him. For that was what the interview had been. That was why Hugo had made him watch.

By the end of the interview it was made very clear that this would be the only time they would talk of it; that they believed their explanation and apologies were done. A great big line had been drawn under the day Sadie left Hugo at the altar. This chapter of the country's history was well and truly closed.

Then it was over.

Will's glass sat in a puddle of condensation next to a very large tip as he dashed from the pub.

Outside, he had no idea which way to turn. He grabbed his phone, jabbed in Hugo's number.

Hugo answered on the first ring. "Hey, mate, how's things?"

"Where is she?" Will asked, walking just to feel as though he was going somewhere.

"Now he's in an all fire rush—"

"Hugo."

Hugo chuckled. "She moved out of the palace the day she came back."

"What's her mother's new address?"

"She's not there either. For now she's taken a room in that dilapidated old hovel you holed her up in for those first couple of days."

And suddenly Will was running, scooting around people blocking his way, leaping over a display of boxes holding masses of pink flowers. His shoes slapped against the uneven pavement, his jacket and scarf flying out behind him.

"Probably a good time to tell you I'm heading away for a while."

Will made a left, realised he'd taken a wrong turn. Spinning on his heel, he made a right instead. "Where are you going?"

"Not sure it matters right now. I just wanted you to know so if you don't hear from me you understand why."

Reading between the lines, Will knew: Hugo had taken the olive branch.

Will turned the corner to find himself facing La Tulipe. The window to the Tower Room was open, the gauzy curtain flapping in the wintry breeze.

His lungs burned from the icy air. His neck itched from the heat of the woollen scarf. And as he shook out his cold fingers he realised he'd left his laptop, his notes, his life's work behind in the pub.

The fact that he felt zero compunction to leave this spot to collect his all-important work was final proof of how fundamentally his world view had broadened. Made room for diversion, for insouciance, for the contents of the room above. And it would still be there when he got around to picking it up. This was Vallemont, after all.

Will breathed out fast and hard. The last of his breath leaving on a laugh.

"Everything all right, Darcy?" Hugo asked over the phone.

"It's been a big few days."

"Tell me about it."

"Promise me something. Next time you agree to marry a girl, you actually go through with it."

Hugo laughed. "I don't think that will be a problem I will ever have to face again."

After a loaded beat, Hugo hung up.

Will put the phone in his pocket and stared up at the open window.

She had left. And he had let her go. Because when you lose enough of the people you love, letting people go became a fallback position.

Only here he was. Because he'd been looking at it all wrong.

Gravity wasn't entirely destructive. It helped hold the entire universe together.

Looking around, he picked up a small stone. He threw it towards the window, hearing it skitter across the balcony floor.

A few seconds later he picked up another and tried again. This time the stone hit the glass door.

His heart was thundering in his chest by that stage, as if it were trying to kick its way through his ribs.

Then the door moved, the curtains sucking inside the room.

And there she was. Beneath a fluffy pink beanie with a pompom on top, her hair bobbed on her shoulders. Her lips were painted a pretty pale pink. A dark floral dress flared at her wrists and landed just above her knees. Brown tights disappeared into knee-high boots.

"Sadie."

"Quite the aim you have."

"Had to do something when we skipped out on school. Skimming stones at a local lake was right up there."

Her hands gripped the railing. "Were you just passing through?"

"I was, in fact, enjoying a quiet beer in a pub down the way when I saw you on the television."

"You did?" She licked her lips. "Was it any good? I couldn't bring myself to watch."

He moved closer to the building, so that he could see her better. "I liked your hair clip."

Her hand moved to her beanie, her cheeks pinking.

"I do have one question for you though."

She leant her arms against the railing. "What's that?"

"It was Reynaldo behind the Templeton Grant. And you were the one behind Reynaldo."

"That's not a question."

"How on earth did you swing it?"

"Prince Reynaldo put the hard word on a friend

of mine once. I figured it was time someone did the same back to him."

"What did you give up in return?"

A slow grin spread across her face. "A promise to never again agree to marry anyone in his family. It was a difficult decision but in the end I felt it was the right one for me."

"Not only for you," he said.

She breathed out hard and fast. Her smile was open and warm, and just like that he let it in. He let her in. Let her fill him up. Take him over. And it was as if he'd opened his eyes fully for the first time in his life.

Had the sky been that blue a moment before? The buildings that many shades of yellow? Did winter ever smell this good?

Will could no longer feel his feet. It was as if gravity had simply stopped working. Only one way to be sure—he moved closer to the building and took a better look at the bricks. He grabbed hold of a couple and gave them a wiggle.

"What do you think you're doing?" she called. "Do not climb up that wall!"

A beat, then, "Well, I can't go in the front door. Janine will see me. And then she'll start quoting *Much Ado About Nothing*. Or she'll want to know how I know the Prince, and I'll never get out of there—"

"Sod it," said Sadie, tossing a leg over the edge of the balcony.

What? No. "You have to be kidding."

"I'm no damsel in distress, remember."

Right. It didn't stop him from standing beneath her with his arms outstretched, ready to catch.

A few of the bricks had seen better days, sending sprays of crumbing shale to hit the ground and turn to dust. But she made it down, feet first, pulling bougainvillaea flowers from the front of her dress.

"You quite done?" he asked, his voice rough.

She looked at him then, her eyes full, her whole body quaking with the kind of energy that could no doubt be seen from outer space.

Then she was in his arms before he even knew they were moving. The scent of honeysuckle filled his senses, and the grey blah that had held him in its grip the past few days melted away.

And then he took her face in his hands, her sweet, lovely face, and he kissed her. And kissed her. And kissed her. "I should never have let you go. No. Let me start again."

"I thought you started pretty well," she said, her voice a husky croak.

"I was right to let you go. For you can go wherever the hell you want, whenever the hell you want. What I mean is, I should never have let you go without telling you what you have come to mean to me."

"Okay."

"I'm used to being alone."

"Big shock."

He should have known she wouldn't make this easy. But that was what he loved about her.

What he *loved* about her. *He loved her.* Where first there was something that took up no space at all, suddenly he was inundated. Because he, a man who believed in things he could see, measure and explain, was in love.

"What I am trying to say, if you'll shut up and let me, is that I'm used to being alone, the way you are used to being surrounded. Your life is here. Mine is everywhere else. You are an untidy grub—"

"While you are so fastidious I don't know how you manage to leave the house in the morning." Sadie blinked up at him, all sleepy-eyed, as her fingers curled into his hair, tugging at the ends every few seconds, sending shards of electricity right through him.

Screw it.

"I love you, Sadie."

The twirling stopped.

"I am in love with you. I have all the evidence to back it up too. Physical, intellectual, anecdotal. But I don't care. The only important thing is that I feel it, right here."

He slapped a hand over his heart and wished with every ounce of his being that she might believe him. Then, with a rush of inspiration that could only have come from somewhere beyond the realm of his understanding, he brought out the big guns. *"Doubt thou the stars are fire; Doubt that the sun doth move; Doubt truth to be a liar; But never doubt I love."*

A little *Hamlet* right when it counted. She grinned and laughed, tears now streaming down her face. "I don't doubt. I believe it," she said. "I believe you."

To think this alternative reality had been out there in the universe all this time and he'd closed himself off to it. He chided himself as a man of science and vowed to explore every angle of this new discovery.

Starting with Sadie's mouth. Her soft, pink, delicious mouth. The sweetest taste there was.

After an age, she pulled away, straining for breath as she rested her head against his chest. "I love you too, you know."

Will tipped her chin so he could look into her eyes. "I didn't actually. But that is good to know."

She grinned, the grin turning into laughter. Then she let him go, flinging her arms out sideways, tipping her head to the sun. "I'm totally, madly in love with you. Which is crazy, right? That this happened. Imagine if Hugo and I had never come up with our fool plan. Imagine if we'd come to our senses earlier. Imagine if I'd never run. The chances were high that we'd have never met. There's only one possible explanation for it. This was always in the stars."

"Sadie."

"Yes, Will," she said on a sigh as she brought her hands to his shoulders.

"As a man of science, I'm going to pretend I didn't hear a word you said past 'madly in love'. Okay?"

"You do what you need to do. Just know that I do love you. Physically." She lifted onto her toes to place a kiss at the corner of his mouth. "Intellectually." She dragged a kiss over the edge of his jaw. "Anecdotally." With that she bit down on his earlobe.

"Good afternoon."

Sadie slowly edged her teeth away from Will's ear before as one they turned to look over Sadie's shoulder.

A local baker was riding by on his bicycle, a bag of baguettes poking out of the basket at the back. He gave them a jaunty wave.

"Good afternoon," they said as one.

"Just saw your interview on the TV," said the baker, letting his foot drift to the pavement as he pulled to a stop. "Very nicely handled. If the rest of your generation is as savvy as our Prince, then our country is in for a grand future. Now you can hopefully get on with your lives."

Will's hand drifted to Sadie's lower back right as her hand curled around the back of his neck. She said, "Sounds like a plan to me."

With that the baker sat back onto his bike and rolled down the hill, whistling as he went.

Will pressed his lips against Sadie's ear. "Shall we? Get on with our lives?"

She plucked a purple flower from his shoulder, then smiled into his eyes. "Let's."

EPILOGUE

SADIE WOKE UP. Sensing it was still the middle of the night, she thought about rolling over and going back to sleep but instead she stretched, hands and feet reaching for the four corners of her glorious, big new bed.

It took up the entire platform in her bedroom in the Tower Room at La Tulipe. No canopy, no fake ivy, no net curtains. Nothing princessy about it at all.

She'd bought the bed for Will as a gift when they'd moved in. He'd bought her the building to put it in, so fair was fair.

She let her hands and feet relax, her breaths slowing, a smile spreading over her face as she thought about her plans for the coming day.

There was a meeting with the architect and project manager first thing, as refurbishment was beginning in the old foyer next week—the administration offices of the brand-new Vallemont Royal Youth Theatre Company.

As patron, Hugo had requested something dry, esoteric, modern for their first play. As chief financial officer, Natalie had told Hugo to keep his intellectual nose out of things he didn't understand. As front office manager, Janine hadn't stopped smiling long enough to have a decided opinion. As director, Sadie had smiled and nodded and told everyone she'd certainly take his thoughts into consideration.

Rehearsals for *Romeo and Juliet* began that afternoon.

As for the rest of La Tulipe—it would eventually become home. So far, they were living out of the Tower Room and would do for some time. The place was crumbling, with so many add-ons and temporary walls built over the years it would be like a puzzle to undo it all and bring it back to its former glory. But they had time. Years. Their whole lives.

She breathed in deeply and rolled over, ready for sleep to come again.

But something stopped her.

Her eyes sprang open. She sat bolt upright. Weak moonlight poured into the room and she struggled to make out shapes in the semi-darkness. There! By the couch. The overnight bag on the floor.

Will was home.

Sadie leapt out of bed and wrapped a robe around herself—black, soft, Will's—then padded out to the balcony. The night was crystal-clear. The moon a sliver in the sky.

She climbed the new stepladder that had been bolted to the side of the tower, used the turrets to haul herself over the top and landed with her usual lack of finesse.

And there he sat, rubbing a hand over his beard as he finessed the mighty new telescope that took up half the roof. Maia had been retired to their London pad and lived in her own custom-built glassed-in, rooftop conservatory, for ever pointing at the sky.

Will looked up at the reverberation of her landing. He pressed back into the seat and rubbed the eye that had been pressed against the lens. His voice was a familiar deep, wonderful rumble as he said, "Hey."

She couldn't hold back. She ran. And she leapt. He caught her, strong enough not to topple as she launched herself at him.

"When did you get back?" she asked, her voice muffled by the fact she was nestled into his neck.

"An hour ago."

"Why didn't you wake me?"

"You know how you are."

"Like a Labrador puppy, all energy then…deep, deep sleep; yeah, I know. How was the trip?"

Will had spent three days lecturing on his beloved Orion Nebula at Boston University, had hosted an international day of moon-viewing from the northern tip of Alaska, then had headed to London to record a voice-over for a BBC documentary. And it sat so well on him, he looked as if he'd just woken from eight perfect hours of sleep.

The man was a natural phenomenon. No wonder the whole world wanted a piece of him. Thankfully Sadie had grown up with a best friend who was a wanted man. She'd learned to be a good sharer.

"Good," he said. "Great. Some brilliant young minds out there giving me a run for my money. I might even have found the first recipient of the new and improved Templeton Grant."

"Oh, Will, that's so cool."

"Isn't it just?" Will lifted a hand to push Sadie's hair from her face.

Her heart skittered in her chest at his touch. She wondered if it always would. She figured there was a pretty good chance.

She settled on his lap, wrapped her arms about his neck and kissed him. Or he kissed her. They probably met somewhere in the middle, which seemed to be their way, and that was her last thought as sensation took over. Her body was all melting warmth, the chill of the night air a distant memory as they too made up for lost time.

Light years later they pulled apart, Sadie sighing. "Now get back to work. All that data won't record itself. I'll just sit here quietly and do my best not to disturb you." With that she sank her head against his chest.

"I'm not sure my calculations will be entirely reliable."

"No? How about if I do this?" She wriggled a little more until she was sure she was getting the reaction she was after.

Will picked her up as he stood. She laughed, and clung to his neck, as he stepped out of the chair, her voice carrying off into the night, over the top of the village that was now her home—

their home—dissipating long before it reached the mountains beyond.

And out there, dark beneath the bright white caps of snow above, the palace slept.

Its story no longer her own.

"Oh?" she said, feigning surprise. "You done for the night?"

"Not even close," Will rumbled as he dropped her feet to the cold stone floor.

He chased her down the ladder and took her to bed, where he made her see stars.

* * * * *

LET'S TALK

Romance

For exclusive extracts, competitions
and special offers, find us online:

f facebook.com/millsandboon

⊙ @millsandboonuk

🐦 @millsandboon

Or get in touch on 0844 844 1351*

For all the latest titles coming soon,
visit millsandboon.co.uk/nextmonth

Want even more
ROMANCE?

Join our bookclub today!

'Mills & Boon books, the perfect way to escape for an hour or so.'

Miss W. Dyer

'Excellent service, promptly delivered and very good subscription choices.'

Miss A. Pearson

'You get fantastic special offers and the chance to get books before they hit the shops'

Mrs V. Hall

Visit millsandbook.co.uk/Bookclub and save on brand new books.

MILLS & BOON